Enjoy all of these American Girl Mysteries

THE SILENT STRANGER   A *Kaya* Mystery

LADY MARGARET'S GHOST   A *Felicity* Mystery

TRAITOR IN THE SHIPYARD   A *Caroline* Mystery

SECRETS IN THE HILLS   A *Josefina* Mystery

THE RUNAWAY FRIEND   A *Kirsten* Mystery

THE HAUNTED OPERA   A *Marie-Grace* Mystery

THE CAMEO NECKLACE   A *Cécile* Mystery

SHADOWS ON SOCIETY HILL   An *Addy* Mystery

CLUE IN THE CASTLE TOWER   A *Samantha* Mystery

A GROWING SUSPICION   A *Rebecca* Mystery

INTRUDERS AT RIVERMEAD MANOR   A *Kit* Mystery

CLUES IN THE SHADOWS   A *Molly* Mystery

LOST IN THE CITY   A *Julie* Mystery

*and many more!*

— A *Caroline* MYSTERY —

# THE TRAVELER'S TRICKS

by Laurie Calkhoven

★ American Girl®

Special thanks to Judy Woodburn

Published by American Girl Publishing
Copyright © 2014 American Girl

Questions or comments? Call 1-800-845-0005, visit **americangirl.com**,
or write to Customer Service, American Girl, 8400 Fairway Place,
Middleton, WI 53562-0497.

Printed in China
14 15 16 17 18 19 20 LEO 10 9 8 7 6 5 4 3 2 1

PICTURE CREDITS
The following individuals and organizations have generously
given permission to reprint illustrations contained in "Looking Back":
pp. 168–169—© Carl D. Walsh/Aurora Photos/Corbis (coach at inn);
The Connecticut Historical Society, Hartford, Connecticut. Gift of
Nancy Phelps (Mrs. John A.) Blum, Jonathan Phelps Blum, and Timothy
Alexander Blum (Phelps' Inn sign); pp. 170–171—*East Side Market Street from
Maiden Lane South, Albany, 1805*, James Eights (1798–1882), 1805, watercolor
on paper, ht. 12 x w. 19 3/8 inches, Albany Institute of History & Art, bequest of
Ledyard Cogswell, Jr., 1954.59.68; © The Metropolitan Museum of Art/
Art Resource, NY (yellow stagecoach); North Wind Picture Archives (coach
entering forest); New Hampshire Historical Society (leather dispatch case);
pp. 172–173—*The Pemigewasset Coach* by Enoch Wood Perry, © Shelburn Museum,
Shelburne, Vermont (rear view of coach); New Hampshire Historical Society
(J. George tavern sign); *Fairview Inn*, © Enoch Pratt Free Library, Maryland's
State Library Resource Center. All rights reserved. Used with permission.
Unauthorized reproduction or use prohibited; pp. 174–175—John Lewis Krimmel
(American, 1786–1821), *Village Tavern, 1813–14*, oil on canvas, 16 7/8" x 22 1/2",
Toledo Museum of Art (Toledo, Ohio), purchased with funds from the
Florence Scott Libbey Bequest in Memory of Her Father, Maurice A. Scott,
1954.13, Photo Credit: Photography Incorporated, Toledo; New Hampshire
Historical Society (elephant ad); The Colonial Williamsburg Foundation.
Museum Purchase (magic show).

Illustrations by Sergio Giovine

Cataloging-in-Publication data
available from the Library of Congress

*For Josanne*
*with love and thanks*

# TABLE OF CONTENTS

# A JOURNEY BEGINS

When Caroline Abbott woke, it was still dark, and her room was so cold that her breath made a little puff of vapor when she yawned. She shivered and tugged her quilt up to her nose but felt too excited even to shut her eyes again. It seemed like forever before she heard a quiet knock on her door, followed by her mother's soft voice.

"It's time," Mama said.

"I'm awake," Caroline whispered, sitting up.

"I'll be in the kitchen," Mama whispered back. "Dress quickly."

Caroline shook her friend Rhonda Hathaway until the sleepy girl sat up with a groan. "What time is it?" she asked.

"Three o'clock," Caroline answered.

"Why do stagecoaches have to leave so early?" Rhonda moaned.

Caroline was too enthusiastic to share Rhonda's complaints. In exactly an hour, she was going to do something she had never done before—ride on a stagecoach! In fact, today would be the start of so many "firsts" that she wasn't sure she could even count them. It would be the first time she had traveled so far from home, the first time she would stay at an inn, and the first time she would visit a real city—the bustling city of Albany, New York. Rhonda had done most of these things many times.

Before coming to Sackets Harbor, Rhonda and her family had lived in Albany. Her father, an army officer, had been sent to Sackets Harbor after the United States declared war on Great Britain in June of 1812. Rhonda, her little sister Amelia, and their mother had come, too, and had moved into the Abbotts' house. The Hathaways often visited friends and relatives in Albany. Today, Rhonda was going again—and taking Caroline with her!

The two girls washed and dressed quickly in the clothes they had laid out the night before. By the time Caroline had pulled on her thick woolen socks, two flannel petticoats, and her warmest dress, she felt a little squeezed, but she quickly forgot her discomfort when she headed downstairs. Just seeing her carpetbag alongside Rhonda's leather valise at the door, ready to be carried to the inn where the stagecoach waited, sent a tingle of excitement down her spine.

The whole family had gotten up to see the girls off. Mama and Grandmother were in the kitchen making breakfast. Papa sat at the table sipping coffee. Even Inkpot, Caroline's black cat, weaved around her ankles.

The bacon sizzling over the fire smelled so delicious that, despite her nervous excitement, Caroline was suddenly hungry. "Won't the stagecoach stop for breakfast?" she asked.

"Not for two hours at least," Papa said.

"I want you girls to have good, hot food in your stomachs to keep you warm," Grandmother added, putting fresh-out-of-the-oven biscuits on the table. "It's going to be a cold trip."

"We're awfully bundled up," Caroline said, patting the thick layers of clothing at her waist.

"Caroline," Papa said with a smile, "you've barely been home and now you leave us again. Traveling on a stagecoach like a grown-up young woman. You'll be so worldly when you return, I may not recognize you."

"Oh, Papa," Caroline said, smiling too. "You know I'll miss you." It seemed as if she had barely returned to Sackets Harbor from her cousin Lydia's farm before she had to set out again. Caroline hated to leave Mama, Papa, and Grandmother again so quickly, but both trips were important. She had helped Uncle Aaron and Lydia with the fall harvest, and now she was on a mission to help Papa.

"Rhonda, we're grateful that you were able to wait for Caroline," Mama said.

Rhonda's mother and sister Amelia had left Sackets Harbor for Albany the week before, but when Mrs. Hathaway learned that Papa had business in Albany—business he couldn't leave Sackets Harbor to take care of himself—she had suggested that Rhonda wait and travel with Caroline.

"I'm looking forward to showing Caroline my favorite spots in Albany," Rhonda said calmly. "I don't mind riding the stage without Mama. I've ridden it twice before. Mr. Danforth, the driver, and I are old friends by now."

Caroline found it hard to believe that her friend could be so matter-of-fact about their journey. Regular stagecoach service between Sackets Harbor and Albany had begun only the year before. But Rhonda, who was thirteen and two years older than Caroline, had already ridden the stagecoach twice!

"And don't forget that Mrs. Potter and her grandson will be on the stagecoach as well," Mama said. "I've asked her to keep an eye on both of you."

Caroline didn't know Mrs. Potter well, although she had lived in the village for as long as Caroline could remember. Her grandson,

Jackson, was five years old and, from what Caroline could tell, a bit mischievous.

"Finish your breakfast," Grandmother said. "It's nearly time to go."

Caroline's stomach fluttered as she slipped into her warm winter cloak and then gave her grandmother a hug.

Grandmother's blue eyes looked intently at her, perhaps sensing Caroline's nervousness. "You'll do well in Albany," she said.

Caroline nodded. "I'll do my best."

Then Mama drew her into a hug. "Write to us the moment you arrive," she said, pulling Caroline's hood up snugly. "And mind Mrs. Hathaway."

"I will, Mama," she promised.

Papa took Caroline's bag in one hand and Rhonda's in the other, and the three of them stepped out onto the lane that led to Sackets Harbor's main street. From the top of the hill, Caroline saw the shimmer of moonlight on the lake. Walking into the village, she marveled at the quiet. The village, crowded with sailors, soldiers, and marines since the war began, seemed eerie and deserted in the predawn hour.

As they passed Abbott's Shipyard, Caroline was comforted by the glow of a watchman's lantern. Papa was the best shipbuilder on Lake Ontario. Once, his shipyard had built sloops and schooners for merchants. Since the war began, his workers had been kept busy building gunboats for the U.S. Navy. It was said that whoever controlled the Great Lakes would win the war, and Caroline was proud that the shipyard played such an important role in the struggle. But that also made the shipyard a target for British spies and saboteurs. Papa's workers patrolled the shipyard every night, keeping a careful watch.

As they walked, Papa took one last opportunity to make sure Caroline remembered his instructions, lowering his voice in case anyone was listening.

"Tell me again what you will do when you reach Albany," he said.

"Go to the foundry and ask for Mr. Brown as

soon after I arrive as I can," she told him. "Then I'll give him the envelope you put in my carpet-bag. Everything he needs to forge the fittings for the new gunboat is in it, including your letter, a diagram with the specifications, and the money for the initial payment. If he requests it, I'm also to give him the model of the ship you made."

Papa nodded. "Be very careful," he said. "After Commander Perry's victory on Lake Erie, the British are more determined than ever to get their hands on U.S. Navy ships and plans. There could be spies anywhere."

Caroline nodded solemnly. She knew that the U.S. Navy had defeated and captured six British ships in September, winning back control of Lake Erie. Lake Ontario, the lake on which Sackets Harbor sat, was now even more impor-tant to Great Britain than it had been before. In spring, when the lake's thick ice melted, the British might retaliate for their losses. Abbott's Shipyard had to finish the new gunboat before that happened.

"I wish I could go myself," Papa said. "But

the shipyard is too busy. We've reached a critical juncture in building the gunboat, and we won't be able to finish our work without those fittings."

"Don't worry, Mr. Abbott," Rhonda said. "I know just where the foundry is. We'll go first thing." Caroline felt a rush of gratitude toward her friend.

"I know I can count on both of you," Papa said.

Before she knew it, Caroline found herself nearly at the stagecoach. Its driver, Mr. Danforth, turned to greet them, holding a lantern aloft.

The driver, a great bear of a man with a kind face, greeted Rhonda by name and immediately made Caroline feel safe. He wore thick trousers tucked into heavy fur-lined boots. His buffalo-skin greatcoat, a fur hat complete with ear protectors, and thick leather gloves would keep him warm in the late-November chill. He quickly stowed the girls' bags under one of the wagon's middle benches.

"Climb aboard!" he said cheerfully, holding

his lantern up so that Caroline and Rhonda could see.

Papa stepped forward to say good-bye, folding Caroline in a tight hug. "Be safe, daughter," was all he said, but Caroline could feel in his words the importance of the job he'd asked her to do. There was so much she wanted to say. Instead, she tried to show in the way she hugged him back that she would not let him down.

"I will be, Papa," she said. Then she took the driver's hand and climbed into the coach.

In the faint light from Mr. Danforth's lantern, Caroline could see that it was really more of a wagon than a coach. It had a long body and four benches, each big enough to hold three passengers. The driver sat on the first, of course, behind the horses. Mrs. Potter had already taken a seat on the last bench.

"Good morning, Mrs. Potter," Caroline said cheerfully.

The stern-looking woman held a finger up to her lips, her brown eyes flashing.

Then Caroline saw Jackson, slumped on one side of his grandmother, already asleep again. Even in sleep, the little boy's mouth was curled in a sly smile. Brown curls peeked out from under his cap, as if they could not be tamed.

On Mrs. Potter's other side sat a young man wearing the heavy white trousers of the U.S. Navy. Seeing the girls, he tried to stand to offer one of them his seat. Caroline knew that women usually took the last bench, because it was the only one that allowed travelers to lean and rest their backs. But just trying to stand had made the young man grimace in pain. One sleeve of his overcoat flapped loose, and Caroline could see that his arm was in a sling.

"Please don't get up," she said quietly, taking the third bench. "We'll be fine here."

"We'd much rather sit together," Rhonda assured him.

With a grateful nod, the young man leaned back and closed his eyes.

Caroline watched with interest as another passenger joined them—an army officer named

Lieutenant Stockman, who asked to take the front seat beside the driver.

While Papa talked with Mr. Danforth, a few navy men gathered near the coach, peering in at the passengers.

"I don't see him," one of them said. "I thought for sure he'd leave town on the stagecoach."

"He could be on the road already, moving on to the next town to steal again," said another.

"With my month's pay and your watch in his pockets," said the first bitterly. "The dirty thief."

The navy men drifted away, preventing Caroline from hearing any more. The words *dirty thief* were still ringing in her ears when the driver climbed aboard.

Just as Mr. Danforth took the reins, a man darted out of the lane beside the inn. "Hold on!" he shouted. "Wait for me."

"Robert Herrick! You're just in time," said Mr. Danforth, smiling.

"I thank you," the man answered breathlessly. "I'm afraid I overslept." He threw two bags over the side of the coach and climbed over the driver and the officer to take a seat in front of Caroline and Rhonda on the second bench.

Then Mr. Danforth raised his whip and, with a flick of his wrist, gave it a loud snap over the back of the lead horse. "Get up!"

As they pulled away in the darkness, Caroline could no longer even see Papa, but she smiled and waved in his direction until the coach was nearly to the main road. When she turned at last and eyed the back of the man who had joined them in such a hurry, her stomach did a nervous flip-flop. The navy men looking for a thief hadn't seen him get on. *Could this man be the thief?*

Thinking about its precious contents, she adjusted the carpetbag at her feet and shivered, only partly from the cold.

# 2
## THE EAGLE TAVERN

Caroline tried to forget her worries as the stagecoach set off, but she couldn't help wondering about the man on the seat in front of her. Had he really overslept? Or was he the thief, hiding until the sailors who searched for him turned their backs?

The stagecoach quickly left Sackets Harbor behind. The thick woods on either side of the road swallowed up the moon and starlight and made Caroline feel swallowed up, too. She could see nothing but blackness on either side of the coach. Even so, the horses kept up a steady pace. They and the driver seemed to know the road well.

The stagecoach rocked on its leather braces as they made their way over dips and ruts in the road. Caroline closed her eyes, breathed in the clear, cold air, and did her best to pretend that she was skimming across the waves on Lake Ontario in her skiff, the *Miss Caroline*. It really didn't feel that different. Once or twice Mr. Danforth even asked them to lean to the left or to the right to make sure the coach stayed upright in a deep rut, just the way Caroline sometimes used her weight to navigate around logs in shallow water.

Sailing always made her feel free, and today her game of pretend calmed her worries.

Now and then Caroline could make out a clearing or the outline of an isolated farmhouse as they trotted along. It was still fully dark when Caroline saw a pinprick of light in the distance, growing bigger and brighter as they drew near.

"Whoa, Jo," Mr. Danforth crooned to the horses. "Whoa, Billy." He brought the stagecoach to a stop in front of a farmhouse. A woman held her lantern aloft and greeted the driver.

"Good day to you," she said.

"Mrs. Kirkland," Mr. Danforth answered. "You must have a message for your sister."

"I do. Please tell her that young Richard is doing much better. The fever broke last night, and he's sleeping comfortably. He'll soon be on the mend."

"I'm pleased to hear it," Mr. Danforth said. "I'm sure she will be, too."

They stopped at the next farmhouse to pass on the news, and twice more to deliver mail, messages, and gossip. Mr. Danforth seemed to be a one-person newspaper. Caroline wondered how, on a long trip, he could possibly remember every message he was asked to deliver.

As the sky slowly changed from black to purple to blue, Caroline's mood brightened too. Now that she could actually see the forest, it felt less scary. Riding on the narrow road through the closely spaced trees felt almost like sailing through a thick fog. Now and then an opening in the trees let in sudden shafts of light, just the way a break in the clouds sometimes did.

When Caroline could see well enough, she

studied the stagecoach more closely. It had a
leather roof, supported by slender poles at the
corners and along the sides. The sides were open
to the air. Rhonda had told her that they would
transfer to a fancier coach for the final leg of
their journey, from Utica to Albany, but Caroline
thought she might prefer this open wagon to
an enclosed stagecoach. She hoped it would not
rain or snow so that the heavy leather curtains
would not have to be lowered. She wanted to be
able to see the world she was passing through.

Mr. Danforth kept up a low, steady conversation with the army officer beside him, but
the rest of the passengers were lost in their
own thoughts. Caroline longed to know what
Rhonda might say about the last-minute traveler, but there was no way to talk without being
overheard.

Instead she studied the man as best she
could from the seat behind him. He had an
unkempt mane of dark brown hair and a
small, pointed beard. His long black cape,
shiny with wear, didn't look warm enough

for the November cold. He slipped his gloves off, reached into his pocket for something, and began fiddling with it. Leaning slightly to one side, Caroline could see that it was a coin. Intrigued, she watched him pass the coin between his fingers, over and under, over and under, over and under. It traveled from between his thumb and index finger all the way to his pinky and then back again. He never seemed to look down at his hand, and didn't even seem to be aware that he was holding a coin at all.

His trick reminded Caroline of sailors and their knots. Papa always said that sailors practiced their knots so often that when they needed to make one quickly, their hands would remember how. Caroline had a length of cord in her pocket for that very purpose. But right now she was content to keep her hands in her warm mittens. Despite them and her warm woolen socks, her fingers and toes had gone from numb to positively frozen.

Caroline was just beginning to wish for a chance to warm up and stretch her legs when

Mr. Danforth lifted his horn from under his seat and blew eight quick blasts. Surprised, she craned her neck to look at the road.

"Is there something in the way?" she asked Rhonda. "Can you see?"

"No," Rhonda explained, smiling. "We're nearing a village. This is our first stop—or stage, as it's called. We'll have breakfast at the Eagle Tavern. The driver blows the horn eight times to let the tavern know that eight of us will need meals."

The horn blasts woke Jackson, who immediately began kicking Caroline and Rhonda's bench and telling everyone that he was cold and hungry.

Caroline leaned forward to get a better look at the Eagle Tavern. The two-story wooden building looked like a typical house, with the exception of the long wooden platform that stretched the entire length of the front of the inn. *That must be there to help us climb in and out of the coach,* Caroline realized.

A large wooden sign hung above the door.

The owner's name, B. Dean, and the year the inn was established, 1809, were painted above and below an eagle with stars and stripes on its chest.

The stagecoach was almost to the tavern's front door when Caroline noticed a young woman and a young man, both in green coats, standing to one side with a valise at their feet. She knew that passengers would join the coach along the way, while others would leave it before they reached Albany.

When the young woman looked at the driver, her eyes widened in alarm and Caroline could almost hear her gasp. She grabbed the young man's arm and pulled him into the shadows. Then they both disappeared around the side of the tavern.

Caroline had barely a moment to wonder what had frightened the young woman before a big man, broad-shouldered and well over six feet tall, strode up to the coach.

"My horse has gone lame," he said to Mr. Danforth, his voice a deep rumble. "Do you have room for another passenger?"

This was worded as a question, but it sounded like a demand. The man threw a heavy black bag over the side of the coach without waiting for a reply. Caroline pulled her feet out of its way just in time.

"Charles Jencks," he continued. "I must get to Albany as quickly as possible. I've been on an important fact-finding mission for the governor, and I must report."

Mr. Danforth nodded as he climbed off his bench, followed by the army officer.

"I'm pleased to have you aboard," the driver said. "But if you're in a hurry, I'm sure you could find a horse to purchase."

The man's high-handed expression slipped for a moment. "To tell the truth, I'm rather tired of riding. I much prefer stagecoach travel," he said. "But," he added with a wink, "let's not tell Governor Tompkins."

He eyed the passengers curiously as Mr. Danforth helped each one down. It took both Mr. Danforth and Lieutenant Stockman to get the wounded sailor onto solid ground. Caroline could see that one of his legs was injured as well as his arm.

Rhonda stamped her feet on the ground. "My legs are as stiff as fence posts," she said with a laugh.

Caroline joined her, marching in place to warm her tingling toes and to stretch her legs. She watched the stable boys lead the tired, sweaty horses toward the barn and saw the young woman peering at them from behind it.

Rhonda took Caroline's arm and pulled her toward the inn's front door. "Come into the warmth," she said. "We'll be freezing again soon enough."

Caroline hesitated and turned to look for the young woman again, but she had disappeared.

*Who is she hiding from?* Caroline wondered.

# 3
## MAGIC

Caroline found herself sitting across from Mr. Jencks as the tavern's serving girl placed platters of bread, cheese, pickles, candied fruits, and cakes on the table. To Caroline, it seemed like a tremendous amount of food, compared with the simple meals her mother and grandmother prepared. Even though she had already eaten Grandmother's breakfast at home, Caroline was hungry.

While most of the passengers concentrated on their food, Mr. Jencks quizzed the driver about the towns and settlements they would pass through and how long the journey would take. He asked many questions about the tavern in which they would spend the night, the size of the village it served, and the wealth of the people who lived there.

Caroline wondered if the man was still gathering information for his report, and she waited for a lull in the conversation to ask Mr. Jencks, "What kind of facts are you finding for the governor?"

The man only tapped his nose and spoke in the same high-handed voice he had used to demand a seat on the coach. "That's a secret, miss. You shouldn't ask questions like that when there's a war on. You never know where spies are lurking, especially this close to Upper Canada."

Caroline felt her face turning red, embarrassed to be scolded in front of everyone at the table.

"Of course, you're too young to know not to ask such an impertinent question, or to be bothered with such things as war," Mr. Jencks continued.

Now Caroline's cheeks turned even redder, this time with anger. Maybe she shouldn't have asked the question, but she wasn't too young to be bothered about such things. The war had turned her family's life upside down—and she had even helped defeat the British in the Battle of Sackets Harbor!

Rhonda leaped to her friend's defense. "Caroline's father owns Abbott's Shipyard, the finest shipyard on the Great Lakes. He builds gunboats for the navy. My own father is an army officer. We may be young, but we know all too well about war," she said hotly.

Mrs. Potter gave Rhonda and Caroline a sharp look, as if to say *Mind your manners*, but Caroline gave Rhonda's hand a thank-you squeeze. In the past, Caroline had chafed when Rhonda reminded her that she was both older and more sophisticated, but now Caroline was glad that her friend had the confidence to defend her.

"I beg your pardon," Mr. Jencks said, nodding to Rhonda and Caroline. "I meant no harm."

Laughter seemed to dance in the man's eyes, making Caroline even angrier. Still, his words were polite, so she could only respond in kind. She nodded, too. "No harm done," she said.

"Where are you girls headed?" he asked.

"We are joining Rhonda's mother and sister in Albany," Caroline said.

"Ah," said Mr. Jencks indulgently. "What exciting adventures await you there?"

Rhonda still seemed to feel it was necessary to defend Caroline. "Caroline has business to conduct for her father," she told Mr. Jencks. "*Important* business."

"Really?" Mr. Jencks said, leaning forward. "Your father must place a great deal of trust in you."

The other passengers were looking on with interest, and Caroline began to worry about how much Rhonda had said. Mr. Jencks was right when he said there were spies about—Papa had told her to be careful for that very reason.

"I'm only to deliver a letter to someone he does business with," Caroline said, trying to seem casual. "It's not important." She pressed her leg against Rhonda's, hoping she would get the message—*Don't say anything more!*

To Caroline's relief, Mr. Jencks had already

turned his attention to the officer who'd shared the front seat with Mr. Danforth.

"And how about you, Lieutenant? Are you Albany-bound?" he asked.

"I'm only traveling to Lowville," the officer said. "I have family there."

One by one, Mr. Jencks quizzed each of the passengers and learned their stories. Perley Annable, the wounded sailor, was going home to Boston by way of Albany. He had fallen from a ship's mast.

"Not wounded in battle," he said, grimacing. "Nothing as brave as that. I have only my own clumsiness to blame. But I hope to get strong again and return to the navy. And if they won't have me," he said with a determined expression, "I'll sign on to a whaling ship. I do love the sea."

Caroline smiled at him sympathetically. She loved being on the water, too, and knew that she would be heartbroken if an accident kept her from ever sailing on Lake Ontario again.

Mrs. Potter and Jackson were going all the way to New York City to visit her sister.

"I'm going to ride a steamship all the way down the Hudson River!" Jackson said.

Mr. Jencks began quizzing Mr. Herrick, and Caroline listened closely. She wanted to know everything she could about the mysterious man who had joined the stagecoach at the last moment in Sackets Harbor.

"I'm traveling to Albany to join a theater troupe for the winter," Mr. Herrick said. Then he reached across the table and plucked a marble from Jackson's nose!

Caroline stopped mid-bite and gaped at the marble in Mr. Herrick's hand. It hadn't really come from Jackson's nose, she knew, but she couldn't imagine where it *could* have come from.

"Did you lose something?" Mr. Herrick asked with a sly grin.

Jackson, his mouth a perfect "O" of surprise, started to blow his nose to see what else he could dislodge, but Mr. Herrick only reached behind the boy's ear and produced a coin.

"I believe this is yours," he said, handing it to Perley Annable.

The young man patted his pocket in amazement. "How did you manage that?" he asked.

Mr. Herrick smiled mysteriously.

"My old friend is a fine juggler and a singer of songs, and his acts of legerdemain are astonishing," Mr. Danforth said with a smile.

"Leger-what?" asked Jackson, who was now scratching his head trying to turn up more coins.

"It means sleights of hand—Magic," Mr. Jencks explained. "How delightful!"

"Do more!" Jackson asked, clapping his hands. Caroline couldn't help hoping Mr. Herrick would agree.

"I'm afraid I have to cut this performance short," Mr. Danforth said. "I'll see to the horses. We set out again presently."

Rhonda and Caroline bundled up and excused themselves to use the privy, the small wooden bulding in the backyard that served as a bathroom. On their way back to the inn, they passed the young woman Caroline had seen earlier. She was alone, wiping away tears as she walked to the front of the inn.

"What do you suppose is the matter?" Rhonda asked.

Caroline shared what she had seen before breakfast. "Something about the stagecoach or Mr. Danforth seemed to frighten her."

"Maybe she and the young man are sweethearts," Rhonda said. "And the coach is taking her away from him."

Rhonda had recently shared with Caroline a letter she had received from a newly engaged cousin. The letter had been full of details about their courtship and the plans for their wedding. As far as Caroline was concerned, the news had made Rhonda a bit too interested in who might be courting whom. Now Rhonda saw sweethearts everywhere she looked.

Caroline shook her head. "She looked frightened, not sad."

"Mr. Jencks will get her story out of her," Rhonda said with a laugh as they neared the front of the inn. "He won't stop until he knows everything. And if she's carrying secret love letters or trinkets from her suitor, Mr. Herrick will pluck them out of her nose!"

Caroline laughed along with her friend, but she couldn't help wondering if Mr. Herrick used his talents to do more than amaze. She recalled again his last-minute arrival at the stagecoach. "Do you think he could be the thief the navy men were looking for?" she asked Rhonda.

"Mr. Danforth seems to know him well and was happy to have him aboard," Rhonda said. "Mr. Herrick must take the stagecoach all the time, from town to town. The driver would know if there was something amiss."

"Mr. Herrick picked Perley Annable's pocket," Caroline pointed out.

"And he gave the coin back again," Rhonda observed.

"But does he always return what he's taken?" Caroline asked.

She was still pondering that question when they rounded the inn to shouts of "Thief! Thief!"

Mr. Jencks stood over his heavy black bag. It was lying on the ground—open.

"Someone has been rifling through my

things," he said, pointing at Mr. Herrick. "And that man, that *vagabond*, was the only one here when I came outside. He's a thief, I tell you. Or a British spy in search of my report for the governor."

# 4

# A NEW PASSENGER

Mr. Jencks and Mr. Herrick stood opposite each other, next to the stagecoach. Anger seemed to whip and snap around them like sails in a brisk wind.

Rhonda and Caroline hung back from the semicircle the other passengers had formed around the two men. Mrs. Potter sniffed with disapproval, while Jackson danced with excitement.

Lieutenant Stockman was about to intervene when Mr. Danforth strode up to the group. "Mr. Herrick has been riding my coach for years. He is neither a thief nor a spy," he said firmly.

"My bag was open when I returned," Mr. Jencks shouted. "And he was the only one in the stagecoach."

"Perhaps the clasp came open when you threw the valise over the side of the wagon," Mr. Danforth said. "Is anything missing from the bag? If not, that will be the end of the matter."

Caroline had to agree, much as she suspected the traveling magician of being behind the thefts at Sackets Harbor.

"I was just about to check my bag," Mr. Jencks answered, somewhat calmed by the driver's steady gaze.

Mr. Herrick handed his own bags to Mr. Danforth. "I invite you to search my own bags as well."

"That won't be necessary," Mr. Danforth said. "Let's first learn if anything has been taken."

"I insist," Mr. Herrick said firmly. He glared indignantly at Mr. Jencks.

"Very well," the driver agreed.

The group waited tensely while Mr. Jencks searched his own valise, shoving its contents from side to side. At the same time, Mr. Danforth opened one of Mr. Herrick's bags. Caroline

watched curiously as he pulled out items for
Mr. Herrick's act—a rope, a tall hat, sheet music,
and other odd-looking things Caroline couldn't
identify. The other bag simply held a few pieces
of clothing.

When Mr. Jencks finished going through his
own bag, he announced that nothing was missing. "But you all should check your valuables,"
he said. "My satchel was tampered with. Of that
I am sure."

The worried group climbed into the coach to
search their bags. Caroline, wanting more room,
handed her bag to Mr. Danforth and climbed
back out of the coach to open it.

Mrs. Potter announced with relief that her
pearl earrings were safe. Rhonda held up her
gold locket, a gift from her great-aunt, to show
that it hadn't been taken.

Jackson hopped from passenger to passenger.
One moment he was marveling at Mr. Herrick's
equipment and the next he was peering over
Caroline's shoulder as she pulled the leather
envelope out of her carpetbag and checked to

make sure nothing inside it had been removed.

"That's a lot of money!" Jackson announced excitedly. "May I count it for you? I'm an excellent money counter."

Caroline cringed and quickly shoved the money and papers back into the envelope. Jackson had just announced to everyone within hearing that she was carrying money! The group already knew who her father was and that she had business to conduct for him. A spy or thief would guess that her papers were valuable as well.

To Caroline's relief, Jackson's grandmother called him away. Caroline decided to check the small wooden box in which Papa had placed a model of the ship he was building. "I don't think the foundry will need this," he had told Caroline. "But I'm going to have you bring it just to be sure. Take care that it doesn't break along the way."

Too soon, Jackson had galloped back and was at her side again. He snatched the model from its crate.

"A toy!" he cried. "May I play with it?"

He pretended to be sailing the ship on a sea of air, making booming sounds for its cannons.

"That's not a toy," Caroline said firmly. She took the wooden ship from him and set it back in its box. Then, as she bent down to put the box back in her carpetbag, she spotted a rolled piece of parchment that had fallen to the ground.

*Who dropped this?* Caroline wondered. Only she, Mr. Herrick, and Mr. Jencks had taken their bags out of the stagecoach. The others had searched their bags inside the wagon. She picked up the scroll and unrolled it to discover that it was a handbill:

## *The Great Nicolas,*
## *Prince of Magic*

*The gentleman delights and amazes with upwards of 100 curious and mysterious experiments with cards, eggs, money, and the like, followed by song singing.*

*The Great Nicolas?* Caroline wondered.
*Mr. Danforth called Mr. Herrick "Robert." He must
use another name when he performs.*

Caroline was about to give the handbill back
to Mr. Herrick when the entertainer, still angry
at being accused, turned to Mr. Jencks. She
folded up the paper quickly and slipped it into
her pocket. She'd return it to Mr. Herrick when
things calmed down.

"I hope you are satisfied, sir," Mr. Herrick
said.

"Indeed I am," Mr. Jencks said with a nod.

"I believe you owe me an apology," said
Mr. Herrick, waiting.

"Surely you would agree that men in your
line of work are not always honest," Mr. Jencks
said smoothly. "There have been thefts in the
area lately. At least one constable shared with
me that he suspected a traveling entertainer."

A knot of concern tightened in Caroline's
chest. She didn't like Mr. Jencks, but perhaps he
was right to worry about Mr. Herrick's honesty.
Why had she opened Papa's envelope where

Jackson could see it and tell everyone that she carried money? She decided to keep a close eye on the magician *and* her bag.

Caroline turned to see the young woman who had been standing by the door of the inn approach Mr. Danforth and have a quiet word.

Mr. Danforth nodded to her, then strode up to the wagon and placed her bag under the rear bench. "All aboard," he said firmly. "We're past our time. Miss Bullard will be joining us."

"Jackson, you'll sit up front with the girls," Mrs. Potter said, nodding to the boy, who was still outside the stagecoach. She made room for Miss Bullard on the last bench, between herself and Perley Annable, while Caroline, Rhonda, and the others climbed on board. Mr. Danforth had just gathered the reins in his hands when Mrs. Potter looked about the stagecoach. "Jackson!" she screamed. "Driver, don't you move. My grandson is missing!"

Mr. Danforth looked over his shoulder. "I helped him up," he said. "Where could the boy have gotten to?"

Everyone looked for Jackson. Caroline spied him first when Mr. Jencks's heavy greatcoat, which hung down behind his seat, began to quiver.

The boy popped out from under the coat, laughing. "I made magic, Grandmother!" he crowed.

"Take your seat this instant," Mrs. Potter hissed.

Mr. Jencks quickly stood, pulled his coat underneath him, and sat on it.

Jackson plopped down beside Caroline with a sly smile. Caroline could see that he had something hidden under his own coat, but she decided to ignore it. She needed to keep her eye on Mr. Herrick. Whatever Jackson had, she hoped it would keep the boy occupied—and quiet. When Mr. Jencks quizzed Miss Bullard as he had the others, she wanted to hear every word.

# 5

## MISS BULLARD EXPLAINS

Caroline waited for Mr. Jencks to begin asking questions of Miss Bullard. But both he and Mr. Herrick maintained a tense silence on the bench in front of Caroline. Lieutenant Stockman, who continued to sit beside the driver, tried to engage them both in conversation, but aside from a few one-word answers and a "Stop kicking, please," directed at Jackson, neither man spoke.

Caroline was about to begin a conversation with Miss Bullard herself when Rhonda turned with a smile and asked the young woman where she was headed.

"I'm going to stay with an old friend of my mother's in Albany," Miss Bullard said.

Mrs. Potter sniffed. "Young women shouldn't be traveling alone."

41

"I'm sixteen, ma'am," Miss Bullard said. "Not so *very* young. And I'm afraid I have no choice," she added. "I'm sure the stagecoach is safe."

"Have you been to Albany before?" Caroline asked. "It's my first trip."

"Mine as well. I must find employment, and Albany seems the most likely place," Miss Bullard answered.

"Employment?" Mrs. Potter asked. "Why would a girl like you need to find employment? What does your mother have to say about that?"

"My mother died five years ago," Miss Bullard replied. "My father passed away this summer. My brother, Henry, and I tried to keep the farm going, but it was too much for us. We had to sell. And so now I need work."

Caroline and Rhonda exchanged a sympathetic look. Mrs. Potter's disapproval surely must have made poor Miss Bullard feel worse.

Rhonda turned to the young woman with a smile. "It *can* be difficult to start over in a new place. But I'm sure you'll quickly make new friends, as I did when I moved to Sackets

Harbor," she said, giving Caroline's hand a squeeze. "You won't be on your own for long, Miss Bullard. Why, I'd guess that soon you'll have a suitor—if you don't already?"

Caroline knew that Rhonda was thinking of the young man who'd been with Miss Bullard at the Eagle Tavern. But Miss Bullard only looked puzzled for a moment. Then she smiled, showing off a pair of charming dimples. "Please, call me Elizabeth," she said. "Perhaps someday I shall be married, but for now my hope is to be taken on as an assistant to a dressmaker. My mother was an expert with the needle and taught me much, but of course, there's always more to learn. I'd like to have my own dress shop one day."

Caroline understood Elizabeth's dream to have her own shop one day. She admired the way Mama worked alongside Papa in the ship-building business, and she herself loved how independent she felt when she was sailing her own skiff, *Miss Caroline*. She loved being able to make all her own decisions about what course to take and how to trim the sails.

Rhonda, however, seemed disappointed by Miss Bullard's lack of marriage plans. "My cousin, who is engaged to be married, was completely surprised by her suitor's proposal. Perhaps you will be surprised as well!" she said encouragingly.

Elizabeth's brow crinkled. "But I have no suitor."

"Then was that your brother with you at the inn?" Caroline asked. "Why isn't he going to Albany with you?"

A look of alarm crossed Elizabeth's face, the same look Caroline had seen when the stage-coach had pulled up to the inn at the last stop.

"My—my brother is in the army, stationed in Sackets Harbor," Elizabeth said. "I was with no one at the inn."

Caroline frowned. There *had* been a young man with Elizabeth at the inn; Caroline was sure of it. She was about to ask again when Rhonda nudged her with an elbow and gave a quick shake of her head as if to say, *Let her keep her secrets.*

Caroline could tell by the twinkle in Rhonda's eye that she still thought the young man might be a sweetheart, but Caroline wasn't convinced. Miss Elizabeth Bullard was keeping a secret, and Caroline only hoped it had nothing to do with the thefts she'd heard about as they were leaving Sackets Harbor.

The girls finished talking with Elizabeth and faced forward again. Whenever Caroline was worried or her thoughts were tangled, she liked to work with her hands. She had no needlework handy, so she pulled the length of rope out of her pocket to practice her newest knot—the French hitch—while she tried to make sense of Elizabeth's falsehood. It was true that a young lady would not want to be seen alone in the company of a young man. Was Rhonda right? Could Elizabeth simply have been trying to hide the fact that she had a suitor?

It wasn't long before Caroline's knots drew Jackson's attention. He quickly abandoned whatever secret he had concealed in his coat and peered intently at the rope in Caroline's hands.

"Are you doing magic?" he asked.

"I wish I could!" Caroline said. "But I'm practicing my sailor's knots. If I ever need to tie one in a hurry when I'm on the lake, I want my fingers to remember how."

"I want to learn!" Jackson said. "Will you show me?"

"This is a hard one," Caroline told him. "I'll show you the square knot. It's the first knot most sailors learn."

Caroline untied her careful line of knots and demonstrated the square knot for Jackson. She guided the boy's chubby fingers through three or four attempts and then left him to practice and tried to enjoy the scenery.

The coach changed horses again two hours after breakfast. Caroline welcomed the chance to stand and stretch. Her back was stiff, her fingers and toes were frozen, and she had grown tired of sitting. Still, when the group set out again she was happy to feel the coach skimming across the road once more. The clippety-clop of the horses' hooves on the nearly frozen road and the birdsong that reached them through the trees soothed her.

She was enjoying the way the sunlight filtered through the trees in a dense patch of woods when she saw a flash that looked like a horse with a rider. *Why would a rider go through the woods,* Caroline wondered vaguely, *when the road is much safer?*

Perhaps what she had seen was a trick of sun and shadow. But there it was again, through the trees—what looked like a horse and a rider keeping pace with the stagecoach. And underneath the sound of the coach's horses and the creak of the wagon, she heard the more distant thumping of a horse's hooves hitting soft ground.

"There's a rider in the woods," Caroline exclaimed. "Perhaps he's trying to catch us."

Mr. Danforth slowed the stagecoach. The passengers leaned forward, scanning the woods. "I thought I saw something, too," Elizabeth said, her cheeks reddening. "But then I realized it was simply the sunlight in the trees."

Caroline turned to her, and the young

woman looked away, avoiding Caroline's eyes.

"I'm sure it's nothing," Elizabeth continued. "Just a trick of the light."

*Nonsense,* thought Caroline. She had seen and heard something real.

The coach sped up again, but Caroline couldn't stop listening for the sound of the phantom horse or looking for a glimpse of its rider.

Then, suddenly, a sharp *crack* pierced the air, making Caroline's ears ring. The coach lurched sharply to the right, throwing her into Jackson and Rhonda, as Mr. Danforth brought the coach to an abrupt stop.

Caroline turned and reached for Rhonda's hand, hoping to see laughter in her friend's eyes letting her know that all was well. But Rhonda's face was pale, and her grip on Caroline's hand was like iron. She was frightened, too.

*Something is wrong,* Caroline realized. *Something is very, very wrong.*

# A PHANTOM RIDER

The coach was leaning perilously to the side. Alarmed, Caroline tried to help balance it with her weight, as she did when sailing under heavy wind. Jackson let out a squeal, and his grandmother practically leaped across the bench to grasp the back of his jacket.

"Will we overturn?" she shouted.

"No cause for concern," Mr. Danforth said cheerfully. "One of our leather braces snapped when the front wheel dipped into a rut. It happens from time to time."

He urged the horses forward, and slowly they pulled the coach out of the rut and onto level ground. Then he helped the passengers down one by one.

"I could use a fence rail for a temporary

repair, but we're a few miles from the nearest fence. Can I ask the gentlemen to search in the woods? We need a strong stick about the length of a fence post—flattish on one side."

"We'll help, too," Caroline said, taking Rhonda's arm. It was a relief to have something useful to do, and it was a perfect opportunity to search for the rider in the woods. She quickly drew her friend in the direction of the phantom horse.

To Caroline's relief, the other passengers followed Mr. Danforth to the woods on the other side of the stagecoach. Jackson, eager to help, pulled Mrs. Potter along with them. Even Perley Annable took up the search, limping behind the others.

"Don't go too far," Mr. Danforth called to Caroline and Rhonda. "Stay within view of the road."

After a few minutes of looking for sticks— and for the mysterious rider—Caroline heard a rustle behind her. She turned to see that Elizabeth Bullard had followed them. And instead of searching the ground for sticks, she was looking straight ahead, scanning the trees.

*She knows there was a rider in the woods,* Caroline thought. *Why did she pretend not to see him? Is she working with the thief who tampered with Mr. Jencks's bag?*

Caroline held Rhonda back for a moment, ready to whisper her concerns as soon as Elizabeth was out of earshot, but just then Mr. Danforth blew his horn, letting them know that a stick had been found and they all should come back to the stagecoach.

The three girls were headed back to the road when a new sound made Caroline jump—a high-pitched, unearthly scream coming from right behind them!

All three girls began to run, tripping over roots and logs in their rush to reach the stage-coach. Caroline could almost feel the breath of a wild, sharp-toothed creature on her neck. She ran faster, holding tight to Rhonda's hand, afraid to look over her shoulder and see what was behind them.

The horses whinnied and began to stamp their hooves. The men raced toward the girls, Jackson on their heels, while Mrs. Potter shouted for him to come back this instant.

"What is it?" Mr. Danforth asked. "Why did you cry out?"

The girls came to a stop, huffing and puffing. Caroline finally looked over her shoulder. She could see nothing but trees.

"It wasn't us," Caroline said. "The scream came from behind us."

"Are you sure?" Mr. Danforth asked. "The sound seemed to come from one of you girls."

"I think we'd know if we screamed," Rhonda said. "It wasn't any of us."

"You girls wait here," Lieutenant Stockman said, "while we search the area."

"Perhaps it was your mysterious rider?" Mr. Herrick suggested to Caroline.

Elizabeth gasped. "Oh, I hope he's not hurt."

Caroline studied Elizabeth's anxious face. *She's awfully worried about a rider she says doesn't exist,* Caroline thought.

Mr. Jencks came striding up behind the rest of the men. "It was probably an animal. I'll search this area to the east to satisfy you," he said to Mr. Danforth. "But the young ladies are fine. We should be on our way as soon as we finish our repairs."

While the men searched the woods, the girls walked back to the coach. Perley Annable was calming the horses. Jackson, who had for once minded his grandmother, hopped about excitedly. Elizabeth leaned heavily against the coach while Caroline and Rhonda explained what had happened.

"I was sure that whatever made that horrible scream was right on our heels," Caroline said. "And yet the men saw nothing."

"Maybe it was a ghost!" Jackson said. He turned to Caroline. "Your horse and rider are *ghosts*."

"Stop that nonsense, Jackson, and stop dancing about," Mrs. Potter said. "There's no such thing as ghosts."

Suddenly another scream pierced the air, this

one from farther away. Jackson's eyes widened, and he dodged behind his grandmother. "It heard you," he whispered.

Mr. Jencks strode toward them, followed by the other men. "Bobcat!" he pronounced with a nod.

"That could explain the scream," Mr. Danforth said slowly. "I've seen bobcats in these woods, and they do sound human sometimes."

Elizabeth let out a long breath. "Bobcat?" she asked weakly. "Could the scream have come from the bobcat's prey? A human?"

"Bobcats generally leave us be," Mr. Danforth said. "You may have startled it in the woods, but it wouldn't have attacked you."

"I'm sure you're right," Elizabeth said, exhaling. "It was simply warning us to stay away. It must have been as frightened as we were."

While the men helped Mr. Danforth replace the leather brace with the stick, Caroline pulled Rhonda aside.

"Mr. Danforth said the scream seemed to come from one of us," Caroline said. "If a bobcat had been that near us, wouldn't we have seen it—or at least its tracks? And yet we didn't."

"It is strange," Rhonda agreed.

Caroline shivered. "Something's not right. And I think Elizabeth's behavior is connected—somehow. She was definitely looking for the rider I saw in the woods earlier. It must be the young man from the inn. But I don't understand why he would follow the coach instead of joining us. And why ride in the woods instead of on the road? It doesn't make sense—not unless they both have something to hide."

"Like the fact that they're sweethearts?" Rhonda asked with a sigh. "What if his parents want him to marry a perfectly horrid girl, and he loves Elizabeth? Or perhaps her brother disapproves of her choice."

"Perhaps they're the ones who went through Mr. Jencks's bag," Caroline said pointedly. "They could be thieves—or spies. I think I'd better talk to Mr. Danforth about this. Something is wrong with Elizabeth Bullard's story, and he needs to know."

She started toward the stagecoach, but Rhonda held her back. "Please don't say anything," Rhonda said. "You have no proof. Think of everything poor Elizabeth has been through—losing her parents, having to sell the family farm, moving to a big city to live with a near stranger and search for employment.

"I feel scared every time we follow my father to his newest army post," Rhonda continued. "And I have my mother and Amelia for comfort. Elizabeth is all alone. That must be frightening enough without being accused of being a thief or a spy. Especially if all she's doing is protecting a suitor."

Caroline knew that Rhonda was right—if not about Elizabeth's having a secret sweetheart, at least about the lack of proof that she was up to no good. Even so, Caroline couldn't shake her uneasy feeling. "At least help me keep an eye on her," Caroline said. "She's hiding *something*."

Rhonda agreed, and the girls headed back to the coach just as Mr. Danforth was finishing the repair. The passengers climbed back inside, the last row first. Once Mrs. Potter, Perley Annable, and Elizabeth were settled, Mr. Danforth helped Jackson up and then Caroline and Rhonda. The girls took their seats on the third bench. It wasn't until Rhonda tried to push her bag out of the way that she let out a gasp.

"My satchel is open!" Rhonda said, her face turning pale. "And my gold locket is missing."

# 7

## STOLEN

Rhonda looked at Mr. Danforth, her eyes filling with tears. "Who could have taken it?" she asked.

Mr. Danforth looked around the stagecoach with a baffled expression. "No other travelers passed us on the road," he said.

Mr. Jencks leaped into the coach and began going through his own bag. He let out a dramatic sigh of relief. "My report for the governor is still here," he said. "You may all rest easy about that."

"My earrings are safe as well," Mrs. Potter said with a satisfied nod.

Caroline swiftly slipped her hand into her carpetbag and checked to make sure her leather envelope was still there. It was, and by its thickness, she could tell that Papa's orders and money were safely inside it.

Relieved, she put her arm around her friend. She knew that Rhonda treasured that locket. "Are you sure it's gone?" she asked.

"It was right on top," Rhonda said, staring into her satchel. "When we searched our bags after breakfast, I placed it there. It was in a blue velvet pouch. Both are missing!"

"It must have slipped down among your things, young lady," Mr. Jencks said impatiently. "Look again." Then he turned to Mr. Danforth. "Perhaps we can be on our way while she searches?" he said.

Mr. Danforth frowned. "We'll wait while the young lady looks for her necklace," he said firmly.

As Rhonda pulled items from her bag, Caroline took them one by one. When the bag was empty, Rhonda lifted it upside down and shook it fiercely.

"My locket's gone," she said quietly.

Lieutenant Stockman had been pacing about

the woods on either side of the road. Now he returned to the coach holding a blue velvet pouch. "This was at the edge of the road," he said. "I'm afraid the locket is gone." Then he nodded at Caroline. "Perhaps the young lady did indeed see a rider in the woods. He could have slipped onto the coach while we were searching in the woods and then discarded the pouch before he made his getaway."

"It was a ghost," Jackson said. "I saw it, too! A ghost horse and a ghost man."

Mr. Jencks ignored Jackson and turned to the lieutenant. "Did you see anything else?" he demanded.

The lieutenant shook his head. "Nothing of use."

"The miscreant could still be lurking in the woods, watching us," Mr. Jencks said.

*Or perhaps the thief is sitting right here in this coach,* Caroline thought, flushed with anger. She shifted her gaze from Mr. Herrick to Elizabeth and back again, trying to gauge their reactions to the theft.

Mr. Herrick looked shocked and concerned, but Caroline reminded herself that he was an entertainer. He might also be a good actor.

Elizabeth seemed sympathetic about Rhonda's loss and, like the rest of the passengers, distressed that the stagecoach had been targeted by a thief. Besides, she *couldn't* have taken the necklace herself, Caroline realized. Elizabeth had been with her and Rhonda from the moment the leather brace had snapped.

Who else could have taken the necklace? Caroline closed her eyes and tried to remember exactly where everyone had been before the scream in the woods had sent them running back to the coach. Her own fear, and the commotion around her, was all she could remember of that terrifying moment. But she knew the other passengers had all been looking for a stick on the opposite side of the road—where Lieutenant Stockman had just found the blue velvet pouch. Could any of them be the thief?

Caroline ruled out Mrs. Potter and Jackson immediately; her parents had trusted Mrs. Potter to look out for her. Perley Annable was too wounded to run or even to walk about much . . . but perhaps he'd stayed close to the coach, and if the locket had been at the top of Rhonda's bag, stealing it would have taken only a moment. Caroline studied the young man, who had winced each time the stagecoach hit a rut, and shook off her doubts about him. Both his injury and his wish to rejoin the navy seemed genuine. They didn't fit the picture of a thief.

But her doubts about Mr. Herrick and Elizabeth were impossible to shake off. Elizabeth hadn't been near the coach, but Mr. Herrick might have been. Or the phantom rider could have been nearby—and Caroline felt sure that Elizabeth and the rider knew each other. Perhaps either Mr. Herrick or the rider had taken the bobcat's cry as an opportunity to steal. In the confusion, the thief might have had time to take Rhonda's necklace.

Caroline longed to sort out her ideas with Rhonda, but even if she whispered, someone inside the small coach would surely hear her.

Mr. Jencks urged Mr. Danforth to get the

coach on its way. "Whoever took the girl's property will be halfway to Utica by now," he said. "We're wasting the governor's time."

Mr. Danforth looked from one passenger to the next with an expression of weary concern. "I understand that you're in a hurry," he said to Mr. Jencks, "but I'm going to have to conduct a search of the passengers. If there is a thief among us, we must root him out."

Mr. Jencks opened his mouth to object, but Mr. Danforth cut him off. "Lieutenant, will you assist me, please?"

"In that case, I insist on going first," said Mr. Jencks. He placed his bags at Mr. Danforth's feet and spread his arms wide. "Please check my pockets as well."

Caroline felt terrible for Mr. Danforth and for Lieutenant Stockman. Both men seemed embarrassed to be pawing through the passengers' things and asking them to empty their pockets. But she had to agree, there was really no choice.

Mr. Herrick kept the rest of the party entertained while they waited. "What have we here?"

he asked, taking Jackson's poorly knotted rope out of his hands.

Jackson watched wide-eyed as the entertainer began to untie the knots. Mr. Herrick then removed a small pocketknife from his pocket with a flourish and began sawing through the rope, keeping up a steady stream of comments about ropes and their uses.

Caroline gasped with outrage and stepped forward to stop him. That rope belonged to her! But just as she found the words to protest, Mr. Herrick closed his hand around the cut and wrapped the rope around the palm of his hand. When he opened his hand again, the rope was whole. Caroline was astonished.

"Again! Again!" Jackson cried. Caroline hoped Mr. Herrick would agree.

Instead, he made the rope disappear—and reappear under the collar of Mr. Jencks's coat! Mr. Jencks stepped back with an angry expression, but through it all, Mr. Herrick kept up a humorous patter. He paused only when it was his turn to be searched.

Caroline held her breath as Mr. Danforth went through Mr. Herrick's things carefully. She wanted Rhonda's locket to be recovered, but she suddenly found herself hoping that it was not Mr. Herrick who had taken it. She couldn't help sighing with relief when Rhonda's locket wasn't found in his bags or in his pockets. Sternly, she reminded herself that, no matter how charming he was, Mr. Herrick was certainly skilled at making objects disappear. If he had stolen the necklace, who knew where it might be?

Finally, after all the passengers had been searched and the locket was still missing, Mr. Danforth cleared his throat and nodded toward Caroline. "I believe Miss Abbott must have been correct earlier, and there is indeed a rider in the woods—one who has targeted the stagecoach."

Caroline eyed Elizabeth, who had led the group to believe otherwise, with a sense of satisfaction. But that didn't bring Rhonda's locket back.

Mr. Danforth opened a wooden box beneath his bench—the box in which he carried mail from one village to the next—and pulled out a large iron key. "I've never had to lock up the mail before, but I think it would be best if you all place your valuables in this box," the driver said. "I don't know if we'll be able to get Miss Hathaway's locket back, but I will do my best to make sure nothing else is stolen."

Mrs. Potter handed over her pearl earrings. "I was going to carry them on my person to keep them safe, but this seems a better plan," she said.

Mr. Jencks pulled a stack of papers out of one of his bags and deposited them in the box. "I must have your assurance that you won't read my report."

Mr. Danforth merely nodded, but Caroline noticed that he pressed his lips together as if he were biting back an angry word.

Perley Annable had nothing to put in the box. Neither did Mr. Herrick.

"Have you anything of value, man?" Mr. Jencks asked him.

Mr. Herrick shook his head.

"Only your talent, then?" Mr. Jencks said.

Mr. Herrick shrugged. "That's for my audience to say."

Caroline wondered what to do with her envelope. Papa had very clearly told her not to let the orders out of her hands until she gave them to the foundry owner, but with a thief about, perhaps it would be best to lock them away. She weighed doing what Mrs. Potter had talked of doing—carrying her valuables with her—versus putting the envelope in Mr. Danforth's box. Which decision would Papa think was more responsible?

An envelope could be lost or stolen if she carried it with her, even if she was being very, very careful. She eyed the wooden box. It had metal clasps and was fastened to the coach's floorboards under the driver's bench. It looked secure. She decided to place Papa's envelope in the locked box. Mr. Jencks held out his hand to take the envelope from her, but Caroline leaned past him and gave it to Mr. Danforth instead.

Mr. Jencks was much too curious about other people's private business. Why, she wouldn't put it past him to open the envelope and examine the contents!

Mr. Jencks turned to Elizabeth, his eyebrows raised in a question.

"I have nothing of value," she said quietly.

Caroline wondered if that was true. If she was working with the phantom rider in the woods, Elizabeth might well have a bag full of stolen goods.

Mr. Danforth locked the box and slipped the iron key into his pocket. Then he picked up the reins and snapped his whip. Once again, they were trotting down the road to Utica.

✦

Caroline tried to take Rhonda's mind off the theft, but her friend was too sad about the loss of her necklace. Soon a gloomy mood settled over Caroline, too. Even the woods took on a melancholy feel as clouds covered the sun and threatened snow. Try as she might, Caroline never caught another glimpse of the phantom rider or heard the horse's hoofbeats. She kept her head turned to the side, her eyes shifting from the thick trees to Elizabeth Bullard, ready to catch the young woman in the midst of giving someone in the woods a secret signal. But she saw nothing odd. Elizabeth had stopped gazing into the trees and kept her eyes trained on the driver's broad back.

At each stage, villagers continued to clamor for mail and news and gossip while the tired horses were traded for fresh ones. Each time, Mr. Danforth unlocked his box to remove a mail pouch and replace it with a new one, and each time Caroline watched him lock the box again and put the key back in his pocket.

Mr. Herrick, who had barely tolerated

Mr. Jencks after being accused at the Eagle
Tavern, now seemed to be the man's best friend.
He stayed close by Mr. Jencks at each stop,
wordlessly following him from the stagecoach
to the privy and back again.

"What is it, man?" Mr. Jencks asked finally.
"Why do you pursue me so?"

Mr. Herrick raised his eyebrows innocently
and pretended not to know what Mr. Jencks was
talking about, but Caroline, too, had noticed
how closely the entertainer had followed him.

When they finally stopped for midday dinner, Caroline was relieved to thaw her frozen
hands and feet by the tavern's hearth, but even
hot food and a roaring fire didn't warm her
mood. She and Rhonda were the only passengers who didn't fill their pewter plates to
overflowing from the heaping platters of bacon
and eggs, broiled chicken, and veal cutlets that
graced the table.

Rhonda played with the food on her plate
and then reached under the table to squeeze
Caroline's hand. "I'm glad your father's orders

are safe in Mr. Danforth's locked box," she whispered. "I'll never stop wanting my locket back, but if those were to go missing, it would be much, much worse."

Caroline squeezed her friend's hand in return. "We'll get your locket back," she whispered.

"How?" Rhonda said. "You heard Mr. Jencks. The thief is probably all the way to Utica by now and on his way to Albany or New York City."

"I don't believe it," Caroline whispered. She looked from one traveler to another, all of them quietly eating and savoring the tavern's warmth before they had to set out again. "I think someone on our stagecoach is involved, and I intend to find out who."

# 8
## TALKING PIGS!

Over the meal, Mr. Jencks kept up a steady stream of conversation, as he had done at breakfast. This time he quizzed Mr. Danforth and the tavern owner, collecting facts about the number of homes and businesses in the villages along their route and about the size and quality of the farms. Then he began peppering Lieutenant Stockman, who would be leaving them at their next stage, with questions about his area of the state. Caroline wondered whether Mr. Jencks was gathering more information for the governor's report or whether being nosy was just one of the man's natural traits.

Jackson, who continued to chatter about ghosts, was the only passenger who seemed to be truly enjoying his meal.

Bundled up against the cold again, Caroline was the first to climb back into the stagecoach. She found her piece of rope, abandoned by both Jackson and Mr. Herrick. She studied it closely, trying to find the spot where Mr. Herrick had cut it in two, but it looked as if it had never been cut. It was the strangest thing, and despite her suspicions about Mr. Herrick, she couldn't help admiring his skill.

As the other passengers climbed aboard and the coach pulled away from the tavern, Caroline began to practice the French hitch knot again. When she had filled the rope, she untangled her knots and began to tie a series of Flemish knots. Tying knots or doing needlework often calmed her racing thoughts and helped her to think more clearly, but today her thoughts remained as tangled as a skein of embroidery thread after her cat, Inkpot, had gotten to it.

She listened to the murmur of conversation between Mr. Danforth and Lieutenant Stockman, and between Mrs. Potter and Elizabeth. Jackson slumped against her on one side, sound

asleep after his big meal. On her other side,
Rhonda was quiet, except for an occasional
sigh. Caroline knew she was thinking about her
locket and the great-aunt who had given it to
her. She desperately wanted to help her friend
find it again. But how?

By the time they reached the next stage,
where they bade farewell to Lieutenant Stockman, Caroline's fingers had grown too icy and
numb to tie knots. Her thoughts were just as
frozen. She couldn't say who had taken the
locket, or how Rhonda could get it back.

As they pulled into their next-to-last stage of
the day, evening was beginning to fall. Caroline
followed the other passengers into the inn to
warm up while the horses were being changed.

The inn looked much like the other inns they
had passed through that day. The front door
of the large two-story house opened into a hall
that extended all the way back to the dining
room in the rear of the building. To the left was
a ladies' sitting room, with plain but comfortable furniture and a blazing fire in the hearth.

Elizabeth and Mrs. Potter immediately walked to the fire to warm themselves. The gentlemen went through the door to the right, to the tap-room, where they would exchange news with the locals and perhaps have a warm drink.

Mr. Danforth stomped into the ladies' parlor, rubbing his hands together to warm them. "It'll just be a minute, ladies," he said. "Then we'll set out again."

"Are we almost there?" Jackson asked.

Holding her own numb hands up to the warmth of the fire, Caroline wondered where Jackson thought *there* was—they would stop for the night at the next stage and then reach the Biggs Hotel in Utica by the end of the day tomorrow. From there, after another night's rest, they would set out for Albany.

But Mr. Danforth seemed to understand what Jackson really wanted to know. "Nearly there," he said. "Two hours after the stable boys harness the new horses, we'll reach our last stage of the day—the Liberty Tavern. We'll have a hot meal and spend the night in nice, warm beds. How does that sound?"

"Good!" Jackson said. "If the beds are comfortable."

Mr. Danforth chuckled and tousled the boy's hair. "Everything that's not a stagecoach bench is comfortable after a long day of riding."

Jackson wiggled and patted his bottom. "That's for sure!"

Caroline was pleased to hear that they had just two more hours of riding today. It was hard to believe that what had felt like an exciting adventure only this morning could so quickly become unpleasant and uncomfortable. Her legs and arms felt stiff, her back ached from sitting, and her whole body felt frozen through. It would take more than a few minutes in front of a fire to warm her up.

She was about to agree with Jackson about how nice a bed would feel when they heard a loud screech from behind the tavern, followed by another and another.

Caroline caught her breath. Had the thief struck again?

# TALKING PIGS!

The taproom door slammed open and men—travelers and locals alike—ran through the dining room and out the tavern's back door. Mr. Danforth flew behind them, followed by Mrs. Potter, Jackson, and the girls.

The tavern's serving girl stood near the barn door, wringing her hands in her apron and looking ready to scream again. The tavern owner's wife went to her side and tried to calm her, but several minutes passed before the girl could speak.

"The pigs talked!" she cried finally. "The pigs talked!"

"What?" the tavern owner, Mr. Wendell, asked. "Mary, you're talking nonsense."

"I came out with some slops from the kitchen, and one of them said, clear as a bell, 'Fine slops today.' Clear as a bell, I tell you!" Mary insisted.

The tavern owner pushed past her and strode into the barn. Curious, Caroline followed him and the rest of the group to the pigpen inside.

"Pigs! Talking!" Mary said again, coming

up behind them. "After the first one talked, the second answered it. 'Wouldn't say no to some apples,' it said. Apples!"

Caroline looked at the pigs in question, their snouts buried in the food. They didn't seem to notice the group of bewildered humans around them.

Jackson nearly climbed into the pigsty, trying to get the animals to talk. "Hi there, piggies. Can you talk?"

The pigs ignored him.

"Talk, pigs!" Jackson demanded.

"Come, Mary, you're a sensible girl," said Mrs. Wendell. "You know pigs can't talk."

"But they did!" the girl answered. "They did!"

Caroline felt sorry for Mary but had to bite her lip to keep from laughing at the idea of pigs commenting on their scraps. She was careful not to meet Rhonda's eyes, sure that the two of them would fall into a fit of giggles if she did. She found herself hoping that Mary's bizarre claims would take Rhonda's mind off the loss of her locket.

# TALKING PIGS!

Mr. Danforth looked around. "Perhaps the stable boys were playing a joke," he offered.

The boys, who had already led the tired horses into the stable and were busy harnessing the new ones, were called to the barn. They both swore that they had done nothing to fool or frighten Mary.

One of the pigs raised its snout, making Jackson jump back with a yelp. Mary's knees buckled. Mr. Wendell brought her a stool, and she collapsed onto it, her face pale. She looked around at all of them. Her eyes widened even more when she spotted Mr. Jencks standing at the back of the group.

"He was here," she said, pointing to the governor's man. "He knows."

Mr. Jencks laughed. "I know no such thing," he said. He turned to Mr. Danforth. "I was on my way back from the privy when I heard her ridiculous screeching. I poked my head into the barn and saw nothing but this girl and these perfectly ordinary pigs."

Then Mr. Jencks turned back to Mary. "I'm

afraid I can't support you in your delusion, dear girl."

"Did you see anyone else? Anyone who could have fooled Mary?" Mrs. Wendell asked him. "She's always been steady. I've never had any nonsense like this from her before."

"I'm sure she's a good girl," Mr. Jencks said. "A boy did run past me as I returned from the privy."

"That's it, Mary—a boy playing a trick," Mr. Wendell said gently. "That's what you heard."

"The sound came from *inside* the pigsty," Mary persisted. "Not outside. You can't tell me that a boy was hiding among the pigs. I would have seen him."

"Then the boy was hiding elsewhere in the barn," Mr. Wendell said.

"There were *two* voices," Mary wailed. "One boy can't have two voices."

"Then there were two boys," Mr. Wendell said impatiently. "No doubt they're watching us now, enjoying your discomfort."

# TALKING PIGS!

Mr. Jencks stepped outside to investigate. Caroline watched him take a few steps and then, still in view of the open barn doors, stop abruptly. Next she heard a laugh, high and light like a young boy's, coming from the direction of the woods. It was followed by a deeper guffaw.

Mr. Jencks turned around and faced them all with a satisfied smirk. "There's the matter settled, then," he said to Mary. "A boy's prank. *Two* boys." Turning to the coach driver, he continued in a demanding tone, "Now, Mr. Danforth, let's be gone. The governor awaits."

Caroline thought Mr. Jencks would stride to the wagon in his usual arrogant way, expecting the others to follow. But instead he hung back and took Mrs. Potter's arm. "Let me escort you, Mrs. Potter," he said. "There are some deep ruts in the yard."

"Mr. Jencks has discovered his manners," Rhonda whispered with a smile. "Maybe Mary was right and the pigs *did* talk."

Caroline giggled. "Two wonders in one day,"

she said. "More unusual things have happened,
I imagine. But it's hard to picture."

Caroline was glad Rhonda felt better enough
about her missing locket to make a joke. The
two girls were still giggling when they rounded
the corner of the inn, directly behind Mr. Danforth and Mr. Herrick. Mr. Danforth stopped
short a few feet from the stagecoach.

"Tarnation!" he exclaimed. "Not again!"

The alarm in his voice made Caroline's heart
beat faster. "What is it?" she asked.

Mr. Danforth stepped aside, and then she
saw—the wooden box had been wrenched from
the wagon's floorboard and was lying on the
ground, smashed open. The mail pouch was in
the dirt next to it.

Caroline's stomach clenched. She grabbed
Rhonda's hand in shock and fear. *Papa's envelope!*
She watched Mr. Herrick lift the mailbag and
feel around inside the box. "It's empty," he said.

The driver dumped the mailbag's contents
onto the ground and sifted through the enve-
lopes. "Your leather envelope is gone," he said

to Caroline. "And Mrs. Potter's earrings."

Mr. Jencks was just rounding the corner with Mrs. Potter, followed by Perley Annable. He pushed his way through the small group gathered around Mr. Danforth. "My report, man!" he shouted. "Where is it?"

"Gone, too," Mr. Danforth said quietly.

"There is a thief among us," Mr. Jencks said. He twirled around and eyed each of them as if they were suspect.

Caroline could barely hear him. Blood rushed to her head, filling her ears with a roar as loud as any gale on Lake Ontario. Papa's envelope—the orders for the foundry and the money to pay for them—was gone, along with a detailed diagram of Papa's new gunboat. In the hands of a thief—or even worse, a spy.

*Oh, Papa!* thought Caroline. *What have I done?*

# 9
## MORE TROUBLE

Caroline was too stunned and scared to speak or even cry. Without the fittings, the new gunboat wouldn't be ready for the navy when the lake thawed in the spring. And Papa's new gunboat design was in the hands of someone who should not have it. Caroline felt like a ship that had overturned in a storm. Papa had given her an important responsibility, and she had let him down. Nothing could possibly feel worse.

Rhonda hugged her. She, too, had no words.

Mrs. Potter, however, had plenty. She scolded Mr. Danforth for encouraging her to place her valuables in a box that could so easily be broken into, and then she turned her wrath on Mr. Jencks for telling everyone and anyone that he carried important papers for the governor. A thief, she said, shaking her finger at him, would take that as an engraved invitation to steal from them.

"I know the governor," Mrs. Potter said. "I met him once at a ladies' tea. You can believe that I'll be telling him all about you, and my report won't be flattering."

Mr. Jencks, who had gone silent during this tirade, only bowed and said, "As you wish, Mrs. Potter."

She didn't look satisfied, but there was nothing more to do. She suddenly lost her bluster and went slack, like a sail that's lost the wind. She stood and watched the men scan the coach and the ground for clues.

"A tool of some kind was used to wrench the box off the floorboards," Mr. Danforth said. "The nails and the metal clasps holding it in place are still there."

Mrs. Wendell urged Caroline and Rhonda to go inside for a cup of tea, but Caroline felt too heavy to move. Leaving the stagecoach would feel somehow as if she were admitting that her things were gone for good.

Mr. Danforth had sent stable boys running in both directions, and for a brief moment Caroline hoped they might find her father's papers on the road. If the person who had stolen the envelope had not recognized the value of Papa's papers, he might have stashed the money in his pockets and dropped the envelope in his hurry to escape. With the orders in hand, maybe Caroline could persuade the foundry owner to make the fittings and wait for payment until Papa could travel to Albany himself.

Caroline felt herself wilt inside when the stable boys returned from both directions, empty-handed and huffing and puffing, to report that they hadn't seen anyone or anything. Soon villagers, too, alerted to the news of the theft, gathered from both ends of the town and reported that they hadn't seen anyone leaving the village. With the exception of the stagecoach's arrival, the road had been quiet.

That meant only one thing to Caroline.
*The thief is one of us.*

She gazed from one worried passenger to

the next, wondering which one of them was lying, which one of them had stolen her father's money and Rhonda's necklace.

Mr. Danforth turned to the group. "I'm afraid that whoever broke the locked box smashed it against the wheel to get it open," he said.

Caroline looked at the wagon and saw that a number of spokes were broken. Splinters littered the ground beneath the coach.

"There's too much damage to the stagecoach to continue today," Mr. Danforth added. "I'll ask the local wheelwright to make the repairs overnight. We can sleep here—if Mr. and Mrs. Wendell have rooms. Then we'll be off at dawn tomorrow, only a couple of hours behind schedule."

Mr. Wendell cleared his throat nervously. "We can certainly accommodate you," he said. "I'm proud to do so. But our wheelwright is away and won't be back until tomorrow evening."

Mr. Danforth took a deep breath and then nodded, resigned to this even-worse news. "That means two nights here. Can you dispatch a rider to Utica?" he asked. "I must send word of our delay."

The tavern owner nodded and then motioned for the stable boys to unharness the horses.

Mr. Danforth began to unload the bags from under the benches. He set Caroline's and Rhonda's bags down in front of the girls. "I will do everything humanly possible to help you get your things back," he said. "The rider will warn the villages between here and Utica about the thief on the road."

"Will you get word to Albany about our delay, too?" Rhonda asked. "My mother will be worried if we don't arrive when we're expected."

"The stagecoach company will send word," Mr. Danforth answered. Then he stood and turned to Mr. Jencks. "It seems that going by horseback is your only option now, if you're to arrive at the governor's on time," he said. "I'll arrange for a fresh horse."

Mr. Jencks looked surprised. "A horse?" he asked. Then, more emphatically, he said, "No! I must use this time to re-create my findings.

Without my notes it will be exceedingly difficult, but I'll give it my best effort."

"As you wish," Mr. Danforth said with a nod.

"I'm glad Mama will be alerted to our delay,"
Rhonda said to the driver, getting to her feet.
"That's one good thing at least."

Mr. Danforth took Caroline's hand. "I feel
responsible," he said. "In all the time I've been
driving this route, we've never had a spot of
trouble, unless you count getting stuck behind
drovers and their flocks of sheep going to market. I felt certain your valuables would be safe
in my box."

The anger and sadness that creased the driver's face made Caroline feel even more hopeless.
"You couldn't have known," she said.

Anger sliced across Perley Annable's face.
"Dirty thief—"

Mrs. Wendell cut him off. "That's no kind
of talk for ladies or children. Come, girls.
Come, Mrs. Potter. And you, too, young man,"
she said to Jackson. "I'll show you to your room
so that you can freshen up before dinner."

She called to the stable boys to help with the bags, but Caroline picked up her own carpetbag and clutched it to her chest, unwilling to risk losing anything more. Then she trudged into the tavern and up the stairs behind Mrs. Wendell and the other passengers.

Mrs. Wendell showed them the ladies' bed-chamber, chatting cheerfully about the quality of the beds and the dinner she would serve, but Caroline couldn't listen. All she could think about was Papa and the promise she had made.

She looked around the room she would share with Mrs. Potter, the other girls, and Jackson. She had never shared a room with anyone but Rhonda and her cousin Lydia. When she thought about having to sleep here with all these strangers—and without Mama, Papa, or Grandmother in the next room—she suddenly felt homesick. Despite the colorful quilts on the beds, the room seemed bare and cheerless.

A fire had already been lit in the fireplace, but the room hadn't yet had time to warm. Elizabeth unpacked a heavy woolen shawl and threw it around her shoulders before going back downstairs to the ladies' parlor, where a fire had been burning all afternoon. Mrs. Potter and Jackson quickly followed.

Rhonda waited for them to leave and then sat down on one of the beds. "You still have your wooden model of the gunboat," she said. "Can the foundry owner find a way to use that to make your father's fittings?"

Caroline's spirits lifted for a moment as she searched through her bag and pulled out the small wooden crate. The model was still inside, but looking at it, Caroline realized that it would not be much help. Even though the model had been carved to scale, Papa had merely used glue for the fittings. She dropped the model back into its box, her spirits dropping along with it. "Even if Mr. Brown would wait for payment," she said, "there's no way he could forge the fittings based on this."

"I'm sorry," Rhonda said. "I know how important it was for you to do this for your father."

Caroline's eyes filled with tears. "I wanted to

make Papa proud, and instead I've disappointed him in the worst possible way."

"Your papa is a kind, reasonable man," said Rhonda. "He will understand."

Caroline knew her friend was right, but knowing that Papa would understand some-how made her feel worse. She wanted to be the reliable, almost-grown girl he could count on no matter what, not a child whose mistake needed understanding. Especially not if it was a mistake that could put Sackets Harbor, or even all of Lake Ontario, in danger.

"At least our room is comfortable," Rhonda said, trying to cheer her friend a little.

Caroline looked around the bedchamber. There were three beds. She and Rhonda decided they would share the one nearest the window, which looked out over the clearing behind the tavern. The moon was just beginning to rise, and she could make out the outline of the barn with its famous talking pigs.

"We all gave the thief a chance to do his work when we rushed to Mary's screams this afternoon," Caroline said bitterly.

"Just as he took advantage of the bobcat's scream to steal my necklace," Rhonda said.

Caroline was thoughtful for a moment. "Both times, there was a distraction that drew us all away from the stagecoach," she said. "Could someone have done that on purpose?"

"But how?" Rhonda asked. "And who?"

"I don't know," Caroline said. "But whoever made Mary believe that those pigs talked did a good job of keeping us all far away from the front of the inn where the coach was. If we find out who did that, we'll find the thief."

"Wouldn't we have heard the noise of the box being broken?" Rhonda asked.

"The coach was on the other side of the inn from us," Caroline mused. "And we all went *inside* the barn. Between Mary's screams and all the chatter, we wouldn't have heard."

Caroline looked out the window at the barn. It was at the very back of the clearing, near the privy, just before the dense woods took over the land. Caroline saw the flicker of a lantern as the stable boys walked back toward the inn, and she tried to remember exactly where everyone had been, beginning with the moment of Mary's scream.

"You still think the thief is one of us?" Rhonda asked.

"I do," Caroline said. "I'm sorry, but I think it must be either Mr. Herrick or Elizabeth. There's something suspicious about both of them. And Elizabeth could be working with the rider in the woods."

Rhonda frowned. "Oh, Caroline," she said. "It just can't be Elizabeth. It's so easy to imagine how much she must care about that young man you saw."

"Elizabeth pretended not to see the horse and rider," Caroline said. "There may be a reason other than the one you think."

Rhonda shook her head with a look that told Caroline she probably wouldn't change her mind. Caroline didn't want to have a dispute with her friend. Right now, Rhonda felt like her only true ally.

"At least we can agree about Mr. Herrick," Caroline said. "There were thefts in Sackets Harbor just before he boarded the stagecoach. Did he really oversleep, or was he avoiding the soldiers who were searching for him?"

"Someone who can do magic tricks must be very good at fooling people," Rhonda said, nodding. "And at making things disappear."

"Like Papa's documents," Caroline said. "Oh, how I wish I had never locked them in Mr. Danforth's box!"

In saying that, she could almost hear her grandmother's voice, whispering advice into her ear. *Such thoughts are a waste of time, my girl. We can complain about our problems or try to change what we may.*

Grandmother was right. Wishes would get her nowhere. The only thing she could do now was try to fix things.

"Whoever stole Papa's envelope is traveling with us," she said, her voice growing stronger. "I'm going to find out who it is—and get Papa's property back."

# 10
# A SNEAKY NIGHTTIME MEETING

Caroline kept a close eye on her fellow travelers as they gathered in the inn's dining room for supper. While they waited to be served, Jackson once again asked Mr. Herrick for a magic trick.

The entertainer patted his pockets with a smile and pulled out a deck of cards. He began shuffling them in elaborate ways, and Caroline couldn't help being amused, despite her suspicions about Mr. Herrick.

He made a card disappear, only to have it turn up in a bowl of apples Mary was carrying into the dining room at that very moment!

Next he fanned out the cards in his hands facedown and had Jackson choose one and peek at it. Although Mr. Herrick never saw the card,

he guessed correctly which one it was!
He did the trick again with Mrs. Potter and
Perley Annable, too. Try as she might, Caroline
couldn't see how Mr. Herrick had guessed correctly. All the cards looked exactly the same
from the back to her.

"Show me how," Jackson pleaded. "I want
to learn."

"I'd so love to learn your rope trick,"
Caroline said.

Mrs. Wendell carried in a steaming tureen
of vegetable soup, and Mr. Herrick slipped the
cards back into his pocket. "A good magician
never reveals his secrets except to a trusted
assistant," he said.

Caroline was a little disappointed. It would
have been wonderful to surprise Papa with the
rope trick when she got home. She suddenly
realized that she had forgotten her worries for
a few moments while Mr. Herrick entertained
them, but thoughts of Papa brought them back
to her.

The group ate the hot meal eagerly after the

long, cold hours on the stagecoach. Mrs. Wendell, with Mary's help, had pulled together a nice supper, and in spite of her worries, Caroline found herself enjoying the way the thick vegetable soup warmed her from the inside out.

She longed to ask Mary about the talking pigs and see if she could find any clues as to who had broken Mr. Danforth's box, but the girl was kept busy running back and forth from the kitchen.

"I hope you've recovered from your fright, Mary," Caroline said when the girl brought in a second loaf of bread.

Mary's cheeks, already red from hurrying to serve the guests, turned even redder. "If it was a joke, it was a cruel one, miss," she said. "Anyone would have believed those pigs were talking. I'm still not certain they weren't."

Caroline smiled and introduced herself and Rhonda.

"It must be so exciting to work at an inn and meet new people all the time," Rhonda said.

"It can be," Mary said with a weak smile.

Caroline was about to ask Mary another question, but Mrs. Wendell called her back into the kitchen. "I want to talk to her some more," Caroline whispered to Rhonda. "Maybe she remembers something that will help us find the thief."

"I hope so," Rhonda whispered back.

Mr. Jencks reached for an apple, nearly knocking over a candlestick with his heavy sleeve. Caroline realized that despite the ample time they had had to warm up, he hadn't removed his greatcoat.

"Are you still chilled, Mr. Jencks?" Caroline asked. "I am nearer to the fire, if you'd like to take my seat."

"I thank you," Mr. Jencks said pleasantly. "But I assure you that I'm warm enough. I'm simply not willing to let a thief take one more thing from me." He reached under his seat and held up his valise to show her that he kept that with him, too.

Caroline didn't blame him for being worried. Still, she couldn't help disliking the fact that he seemed to worry only about himself. She focused her attention on Mr. Herrick and Elizabeth Bullard instead. Though they seemed so friendly, she promised herself she would not let down her guard—she would keep her eyes on both of them.

Mr. Herrick was not doing anything unusual. His mood was subdued, like everyone else's. He resisted being pulled into conversation and put off Jackson's repeated requests for more magic.

Elizabeth, though, was acting strangely. Caroline noticed that whenever the young woman thought no one was looking, she took a piece of bread or an apple and placed it on her lap. And when Elizabeth stood up at the end of the meal, she held her shawl awkwardly in her arms; Caroline realized that it must be concealing the bread and apples. *Why is she hiding food?* Caroline wondered. *And what else has she hidden in that shawl?*

# A SNEAKY NIGHTTIME MEETING

After supper, the passengers headed upstairs to their rooms. Caroline and Rhonda followed behind Mrs. Potter, Jackson, and Elizabeth to the ladies' bedchamber while Mr. Herrick helped Perley Annable up the steep staircase.

By the time they reached the room, Caroline had come up with a plan: She would stay awake and check Elizabeth's things as soon as everyone was asleep. She knew it was wrong to go through someone else's belongings without permission, but Papa's new gunboat depended on getting his papers and money back. She couldn't bear the thought of the navy having to do without the ship when it could be so vital to the United States winning the war against England. The thought of her father's new design falling into the hands of the British was even more chilling. And the thought of the look on Papa's face when he learned the news was worst of all.

Caroline watched Elizabeth tie her shawl

into a bundle and place it on top of her valise before changing into her nightgown and climbing into bed. The shawl would be easy to untie and search once Elizabeth fell asleep.

Caroline felt a flicker of hope. Papa's envelope and Rhonda's locket might already be in the hands of Elizabeth's partner, but if Caroline could bring evidence of stolen goods to Mr. Danforth, Elizabeth might be forced to confess. She might lead them to the person who had Papa's foundry orders and money.

Caroline wrapped a wool shawl over her nightgown and slipped into bed next to Rhonda. She began to whisper her plan in Rhonda's ear but was stopped by the sharp voice of Mrs. Potter. "None of that, girls," she said. "Jackson needs his rest, and so do you."

Caroline looked over at the boy. He was already deep in sleep. Even if the girls shouted to each other, he would probably not wake up. But Caroline only said, "Good night, Mrs. Potter," and blew out the candle on the nightstand.

*Maybe it's better if Rhonda doesn't know,*

Caroline thought. *She's sure Elizabeth is just a girl with a secret suitor. She might try to discourage me from looking through her things. And if I get caught, I don't want Rhonda to get into trouble, too.*

In a few minutes, Caroline's eyes adjusted to the darkness. The moon was nearly full, washing the room with light. Lying in bed, Caroline felt as if the stagecoach were still swaying beneath her, the same way she sometimes felt as if she were still being rocked by waves after a long day of sailing on Lake Ontario. She struggled to keep her eyes open and pinched herself to stay awake as everyone else settled into sleep. Jackson's relaxed breathing was joined by Mrs. Potter's snores. Rhonda turned over and was soon asleep herself. Caroline waited for Elizabeth to drop off, straining to hear her over Mrs. Potter and the unfamiliar sounds of the tavern at night.

Downstairs, the taproom's front door opened and closed. Caroline heard the distant rumble of conversation and the occasional laugh. Finally, even those noises quieted, and Caroline heard the heavy tread of someone—no doubt

Mr. Jencks—climbing the stairs and entering the men's bedchamber across the hall.

On the edge of falling asleep herself, Caroline decided it was safe to slip out of bed. Her eyes on Elizabeth, Caroline began inching her legs over the side of the bed. Her feet had not even reached the floor when Elizabeth herself swiftly stole out of bed and gathered up her shawl!

Caroline quickly drew her feet back under the covers and closed her eyes. Peering through her eyelashes, she watched Elizabeth lean over Jackson as if making sure he was asleep. Then she tiptoed toward Rhonda and Caroline's bed. When she felt Elizabeth's shadow looming over her, Caroline held still. She matched her breathing to Rhonda's, even and gentle. When she finally felt the shadow move away from her, she opened her eyes just enough to see Elizabeth, still in her nightdress, tiptoe out of the room.

Listening hard, Caroline heard the creak of the stairs as Elizabeth made her way down to the inn's front hall. Then she heard the muffled sound of the front door being opened and closed.

# A Sneaky Nighttime Meeting

Silently, Caroline crept to the window and peered through the gap between the curtains. In the moonlight she saw a figure lurking at the edge of the barn. It was clearly a man or a boy, but he was too far away for Caroline to see his face. Was he the young man from the Eagle Tavern this morning—the one Elizabeth had pretended didn't exist? Could he be the rider in the woods?

Without thinking or even stopping to put on her shoes, Caroline raced to follow her. Instead of using the front door, as Elizabeth had, she tore through the dining room and out the inn's back door. She hid alongside the wall until she saw a shadow dart from behind the privy to the side of the barn. *Elizabeth!* Reaching the front of the barn, Elizabeth glanced quickly up at the bedchamber window and then dashed around the side of the building.

Caroline set out at a run across the yard, ignoring the sticks and sharp stones that jabbed her feet, and then slipped around the barn's other side. She peeked around the corner in time to see Elizabeth hand her shawl to the man, who quickly untied it and began to gobble the food. As he ate, Elizabeth talked, gesturing with her arms and pointing to the inn. Caroline could see their warm breath making vapor in the cold air, and she hoped her own breathing wouldn't give her away. She was about to take a step closer when a small wind kicked up, sending leaves skittering across the yard. Startled, she jumped and pulled her head back.

The next thing she heard was rapid footsteps, and Caroline realized that Elizabeth must be running back to the inn. Caroline was about to follow when she heard heavier, slower footsteps. The young man was coming toward her! Had she been discovered? She crouched against the side of the barn and threw her shawl over her head, hoping its dark color would help her blend into the shadows. She held her breath, silently scolding herself for getting into this dangerous position. Why had she come outside by herself? She should have woken Rhonda or Mr. Danforth, or spied on Elizabeth from the window.

With each slow footstep, Caroline thought of one more mistake she had made, one more thing that would disappoint Papa.

The sound of crunching footsteps stopped just feet from where Caroline crouched. From under the shawl she could see the scuffed toes of the young man's heavy boots. He took another step closer and Caroline flinched, afraid that one of those boots was about to kick her. But the young man didn't seem to see her. Caroline heard a loud crunch and realized that he must have stopped to finish eating an apple!

Caroline waited as the young man took several more bites. After a brief silence, the boots turned and the sound of footsteps moved off toward the woods. Caroline did not even have a moment to feel relief before disappointment and frustration sank in. It was all over. She hadn't seen or heard anything that would help. If there was stolen property mixed in with the bread and apples that Elizabeth had wrapped up in her shawl, Caroline hadn't seen it. She had put herself in harm's way for nothing.

Crouched in the darkness, Caroline wondered what to do. Should she confront Elizabeth now anyway, and demand to know what she had been doing? That would accomplish nothing. Elizabeth might warn the man that they were suspects, and he could escape with the stolen property. Caroline couldn't risk that.

Besides, she could almost hear Rhonda's voice in her head reminding her that she had no real proof that Elizabeth had done anything wrong. It was possible that Elizabeth and this man didn't have enough money for two stagecoach fares, and he had borrowed a horse to make his own way to Albany. He could be Elizabeth's brother, keeping a close eye on his sister to make sure she was safe. Caroline had to admit to herself that it was also possible that the two were secret sweethearts, just as Rhonda thought.

Shivering, she waited a few more moments to make sure the man was truly gone. She checked the window of their room to make sure Elizabeth wasn't watching. Then she ran across the yard, her bare feet so frozen that she barely felt them touch the ground. Not stopping to put her shoes on was yet one more mistake she had made. Slipping back into the dining room, she climbed the stairs carefully to keep them from creaking.

As she crept into the bedchamber, the only sounds Caroline heard were Mrs. Potter's snores and Rhonda's regular breathing. Even Elizabeth was back in bed already. Had Elizabeth noticed that Caroline was not in her bed? If so, she hadn't stayed up to confront Caroline. From across the room, it appeared as if everyone was sound asleep.

Caroline wrapped her shawl around her frozen toes and slipped back under the covers. She matched her breathing to Rhonda's and waited for sleep, but it didn't come. She lay awake in the dark for a long while, listening to the wind in the trees outside the window, before finally dropping off.

# 11

# THE GREAT NICOLAS

When Caroline woke the next morning, the room was empty. She stretched, putting off the moment when she would have to push the warm covers aside and face the chilly room. The sun shining through the curtains told her that she had slept quite late. Suddenly she recalled the events of the previous day, and her heart sank like an anchor.

How could she have forgotten, even for one second, that Papa's orders for the foundry in Albany had been stolen? Determined to tell Rhonda and Mr. Danforth about Elizabeth as soon as possible, Caroline jumped out of bed, splashed cold water on her face from the bowl and pitcher on the table, and quickly dressed.

Entering the dining room, she found the

other passengers sitting at a table filled with half-empty platters of eggs and bacon, bread, pickled cucumbers, and candied fruits. Everyone seemed to be enjoying a happy discussion, and Caroline wondered how they could seem so relaxed after what had happened the day before.

Rhonda looked up with a smile. "There you are," she said. "I was just wondering if I should wake you."

"Good morning, sleepyhead," Jackson teased.

Caroline wished everyone good morning, paying careful attention to Elizabeth Bullard.

"You must have slept well," Elizabeth said with a carefree, dimpled smile. "All of our moving about this morning didn't wake you."

"No, not this *morning*," Caroline said, lingering meaningfully over the last word. She waited for Elizabeth to react, but she only passed a platter of eggs in Caroline's direction. *Why does she appear so untroubled?* Caroline wondered.

"There's certainly no hurry to rise today," Mr. Jencks said. "We're stuck here until the wheelwright does his work. Mr. Danforth has ridden off to try to hurry his return. I, at least, have a report to re-create. What will the rest of you do with your time?"

"I'm going to see the pigs," announced Jackson, popping a pickle into his mouth. "I want them to talk to me!"

"And you, my fine fellow?" Mr. Jencks said, addressing Mr. Herrick. "What will you do?"

Mr. Herrick had removed a coin from his pocket and was idly flipping it between his fingers again. He watched Mr. Jencks intently but said nothing.

The coin seemed to give Mr. Jencks an idea. "Entertainment!" he said. "That's what we need. You'll oblige us, won't you?" He didn't wait for an answer. "Innkeeper!" he said, calling to Mr. Wendell. "You'd be happy to host a traveling entertainer to amuse us all this evening, would you not?"

Mr. Wendell began to respond, but Mr. Jencks talked right over him, too.

"Tell the whole village," he said. "Send some-one to the nearby farms. Why, I bet they'll—how do the show people say it?—pack the house."

"Huzzah!" Jackson said. "Magic! I want to see more magic!"

Mr. Herrick seemed reluctant. "Mr. Danforth has gone to consult the constable," he said. "And if the wheelwright returns soon, we could leave—"

"Nonsense," Mr. Jencks said, cutting him off. "Mr. Danforth told us himself that the wheel- wright's work would take several hours, and the man isn't due back before mid-afternoon. Even if he hurries, we'll still be sleeping in Mrs. Wendell's fine beds tonight."

Then he turned to Mr. Wendell. "Think of the customers you'll bring in. Surely you can pay Mr. Herrick something for his trouble. Help us convince him."

Caroline wondered if Mr. Jencks was as loud and bossy with the governor as he was with everyone else.

He turned to the rest of the group. "You all want to see more of Mr. Herrick's amazements, don't you?" he urged.

"Yes!" the others said. "Please?" Jackson begged. Even Caroline found herself wanting the magician to agree.

Mr. Herrick threw his arms up in surrender. "How can I say no?" he said. His mouth was smiling, but Caroline noticed that he looked at Mr. Jencks through narrowed eyes.

"Our village is a small one," Mr. Wendell said. "We don't often have entertainers stop. With the harvest in, we should attract a large audience. I wonder if my taproom will be big enough."

"Why, I'm sure we won't mind supping in the ladies' parlor tonight so that Mr. Herrick can set up his tricks and amusements in the dining room," Mr. Jencks answered.

While Mr. and Mrs. Wendell discussed the details, Mr. Herrick excused himself to retrieve a few handbills from his traveling bag. When he returned, Mr. Wendell gave one of the stable boys instructions to ride out to the nearby villages and post the handbills.

Despite herself, Caroline felt excited by the

idea of a magic show. Maybe Mr. Herrick would do the rope trick again, and she could watch closely to see how he had done it. And she could watch extra closely to see if there was anything in his performance that might give him away as the thief.

Still, it seemed odd that he was so reluctant to perform. Why would a traveling entertainer not want to entertain? Did he fear being recognized by someone who knew he was a thief? Until she had clear proof that Elizabeth Bullard was the thief, Mr. Herrick continued to be suspect.

She was thinking about this when Mr. Jencks, wearing his heavy greatcoat as he had the night before, leaned back in his chair. Beyond him, Caroline could see a man at the other end of the table whom she hadn't noticed before. The man's head was turned away from her, and he was deep in conversation with Perley Annable.

"What say you, seaman?" Mr. Jencks called, getting Perley Annable's attention. "Mr. Herrick will no doubt give us as fine an evening of entertainment as any you could find in Boston."

Perley Annable and the other man turned to look at Mr. Jencks, and Caroline recognized the man's face instantly. He was the young man she had seen with Elizabeth at the Eagle Tavern yesterday morning. No doubt he was the same person Elizabeth had met by the barn last night.

"Ah, Miss Caroline," Mr. Jencks said, seeing her sudden interest. "You have not yet met our newest passenger. Let me introduce Levi Sanborn. This fellow will be joining us on our journey."

Levi Sanborn greeted Caroline with a smile— a smile with dimples just like Elizabeth Bullard's.

Caroline tried not to let her surprise show, but she nearly spilled her tea, dropping the cup onto her pewter plate with a clang. "You—you're lucky you caught us," she stammered, trying to calm herself. "We were supposed to be on the road yesterday afternoon."

"I am lucky, indeed," the young man answered. "I had the wrong schedule, but by happy accident the stagecoach was still here."

Everything about Levi Sanborn—his blue

eyes, his dimples, and his speech—reminded Caroline of Elizabeth Bullard. They *had* to be brother and sister, but why were they hiding it? And why had he been secretly following the stagecoach on horseback only to join them now?

Caroline couldn't wait to talk it over with Rhonda. Rhonda needed to know that Levi Sanborn wasn't who he claimed to be, and that the mysterious rider was not Elizabeth Bullard's suitor. But the travelers, having little to do until the wheelwright finished fixing the coach, lingered over breakfast.

Finally, Mrs. Potter and Elizabeth left the dining room for the ladies' parlor, and the gentlemen moved on, leaving Caroline and Rhonda alone. Afraid they would be overheard, Caroline pulled Rhonda up the stairs and into the room they had shared the night before. Gently, she closed the door behind them.

"Rhonda," she whispered, "I'm more sure than ever that Elizabeth is hiding something, and it's not a sweetheart. That young man, Levi Sanborn—"

"He's handsome, isn't he?" Rhonda said. Her eyes had a faraway look.

"He's not who you think—"

Caroline broke off abruptly when a movement by one of the beds caught her eye. A dark-haired little head popped up from behind the bed and then disappeared again. Only then did Caroline see that the water pitcher on the table next to the bed had been completely emptied into the bowl. Water dripped onto the table and the floor. And there—bobbing in the brimming bowl—was Papa's model gunboat!

"Jackson!" Caroline yelled. She walked around the bed to find the boy crouched on the floor, covering his head as if that were enough to hide him.

Jackson lifted his head and then leaped to his feet. "We're sailors," he said. "We're hunting pirates." He mimicked the sound of the cannons—*Boom! Boom! Boom!*—and then smiled proudly. "We sank their ship. They're drownded."

He pushed the gunboat to the bottom of the

bowl, spilling more water onto the table.

"Stop!" Caroline yelled again. "That's a very important model ship. You mustn't damage it."

Mrs. Potter, who must have heard Caroline's first shout, burst into the room, red-faced and panting from having climbed the stairs so quickly. "What's this about?" she asked.

Jackson smiled sweetly. "I was just playing, Grandmother."

"There's no harm done," Caroline said, trying to hide her anger. She lifted the model from the bowl and dabbed at it with one of the towels that sat nearby. "But I must ask you to leave my things alone. I've told you that this isn't a toy."

Jackson's lower lip began to tremble, but Caroline could tell by the laughter dancing in his eyes that he was only pretending to be sad to avoid Mrs. Potter's wrath.

"You shouldn't leave such things about to tempt him," Mrs. Potter said. "He's a little boy."

"I didn't—" Caroline began.

Mrs. Potter had already turned to leave the room. "Jackson, dear, you mustn't touch other people's things. Now say you are sorry and come down to the parlor."

"Yes, Grandmother," Jackson answered. Then he turned to Caroline and mumbled something that she assumed was an apology. He paused for a moment, as if considering something, then abruptly reached under the table and grabbed a small object.

"Here's your sailor, too," he said, thrusting a small wooden figure into Caroline's hands. Then he scampered out of the room after his grandmother, stopping only to turn and stick out his tongue at Caroline and Rhonda.

Puzzled, Caroline looked after him. Jackson had run off so quickly that Caroline hadn't had time to tell him the little figure wasn't hers, or even to ask him what it was. She studied the small carved doll in her hands. It was less than a foot tall—the size of a doll Caroline had played with when she was younger—but it didn't look like a typical child's doll. It had a scowling man's face and wore the suit of a United States sailor.

"What a curious-looking thing," Caroline

said, not wanting to use the word *ugly*. "I can't think of many children who would want to play with something like this. Why did Jackson think it was mine?"

"Maybe it was left under the bed by a previous guest," Rhonda said. She took the doll from her friend, and her face lit up with recognition. "Oh! It's not a little girl's doll," she said. "Mother, Father, and I saw something like it in the theater in Albany once. The performer onstage could make all kinds of sounds, even carry on conversations, with his mouth closed. He made a doll like this talk like an old man." She laughed. "And he made a teapot sing a tune. It was the funniest thing. He made sounds come from all over the room, even though he stood in one place. I think he was called a ventriloquist."

Suddenly Caroline felt a spark of recognition. "Could he make pigs talk?"

Rhonda gasped. "That's it! That's who scared Mary. One of those ventriloquists."

"A person like that could have made the

bobcat's scream in the woods, too," Caroline said. She remembered that the handbill she had found the first day of the trip was still in the pocket of her cloak. She ran to get it and unfolded it for Rhonda to see.

### The Great Nicolas, Prince of Magic

*The gentleman delights and amazes with upwards of 100 curious and mysterious experiments with cards, eggs, money, and the like, followed by song singing.*

And there, at the bottom of the long list of the Great Nicolas's feats, was the word Rhonda had used: *ventriloquist.*

"I found this on the ground when Mr. Herrick emptied his bag yesterday morning. It must be his handbill," Caroline said. "He's one of those ventriloquists."

"If this is his handbill, then the doll is surely

his," Rhonda said. "But how on earth did Jackson get Mr. Herrick's doll?"

"Maybe it fell out when Mr. Herrick emptied his bag, just as the handbill did," Caroline said thoughtfully. Then her eyes flashed. "Remember when Mrs. Potter thought we were about to leave without Jackson? He was hiding under the bench in front of us—the one where Mr. Herrick sat with Mr. Jencks. Jackson had something then— something hidden under his coat. It must have been this doll."

"Mr. Herrick could have been the one to play the trick on Mary," Rhonda said.

"And if he's just an entertainer, why wouldn't he want everyone to know that he had done it?" Caroline asked. "He must have been up to no good."

"It does seem suspicious," Rhonda agreed. "I'll be glad if we can prove that Mr. Herrick broke into the box. Then we'll know Elizabeth isn't the thief. They can't *both* be guilty."

Caroline frowned. "Maybe not," she said slowly. "But even if Mr. Herrick turns out to be the thief, Elizabeth must be guilty of something." She told her friend what had happened the night before and shared her conviction that Levi Sanborn was not who he claimed to be.

Rhonda stared at her friend, open-mouthed. "You followed her? Why, you could have been caught—and hurt!"

"I know it was dangerous," Caroline admitted. "But I've just got to get Papa's papers back."

Rhonda looked at Caroline searchingly. "Oh, Caroline, this has gotten frightening. Please, let's get help. I couldn't bear it if you were hurt."

"I've already decided to talk to Mr. Danforth the minute he's back," Caroline said. "Let's find out which direction he went in. We can walk to the edge of the village to wait for him."

"Good idea," Rhonda said with relief.

Caroline slipped the doll under her pillow along with the handbill. They were halfway down the stairs when they saw Levi Sanborn leave the ladies' parlor and walk toward the dining room. A moment later, they heard the back door open and close.

"Maybe we should see what he's up to," Caroline whispered. She was about to take another step when Elizabeth, her shawl wrapped around her shoulders, stepped out of the ladies' parlor, too. Caroline ducked behind the railing and watched Elizabeth look around, as if to see whether anyone was watching. Then the young woman set off after Levi Sanborn.

"Let's follow," Caroline whispered.

Rhonda shook her head, concern in her brown eyes. "I'd feel better if Mr. Danforth was with us."

"There's no time," Caroline whispered. "They could be passing Papa's papers on to a spy right now."

Grabbing Rhonda's hand, she set off to catch a pair of thieves.

# 12

# ONE SECRET REVEALED

As quietly as they could, Caroline and Rhonda ran down the stairs and into the dining room. Through the window they saw Elizabeth set off into the yard and stride toward the privy.

"She's only going to the privy," Rhonda whispered.

"Wait," Caroline said, watching.

Elizabeth opened the privy's wooden door and looked over her shoulder. Instead of going inside, she let it close with a bang and then slipped around the side of the privy.

"She's definitely trying to hide something," Caroline said. She dashed out of the dining room and into the yard, stopping only when she reached the privy. Rhonda was right behind her. Catching her breath, Caroline peered around the corner. She didn't see Elizabeth or Levi, but she could hear whispering behind the privy.

Slowly, carefully, her heart beating wildly, Caroline inched along the side of the privy and listened.

"I've made up my mind," Levi was saying. "It's no use trying to talk me out of it. As soon as you're safely in the hands of Mrs. Vandekerk, I'm going back."

Elizabeth's voice was so soft that Caroline couldn't hear her answer.

"I'll face my punishment bravely, like a man," Levi insisted.

"Then I'll come with you and tell them that I lied, too," Elizabeth said, her voice stronger now.

"No, there's no reason for us both to get into trouble," Levi said. "The fault and the punishment are mine alone."

There was quiet for a moment, and then Caroline heard a crinkling sound. Was Levi giving Elizabeth Papa's bank notes?

"Take these," Levi said. "They're beyond value. You should have them."

What was beyond value? If Elizabeth had Papa's gunboat specifications in her hands, she could sell them to the British. Caroline couldn't let that happen! She took a deep breath and stepped into view.

"If those are my papa's papers, you'd better hand them over," she demanded, holding out her hand. "How dare you steal them!"

Elizabeth and Levi were too startled to speak.

Then, to Caroline's dismay, she saw that the only thing in Elizabeth's hand was a small collection of letters tied with a blue ribbon.

Levi threw his shoulders back and looked Caroline square in the face. "Those are *my* father's letters," he spat. "Letters sent to me after I joined the army. They contain his last words to me." Elizabeth placed a hand on Levi's arm to calm him.

As the truth of the situation dawned on her, Caroline's heart sank and her eyes filled with tears. Not only did the pair not have Papa's papers, she had falsely accused them of terrible things. She slumped against the side of the privy and tried to think of what to say. "Then—then why are you sneaking around like this—and meeting in the middle of the night, and pretending not to know each other?" she asked.

Elizabeth looked at Caroline. "So you did see me last night. I worried that someone might, but I *had* to talk to Henry, and he needed food. So I took the risk."

"Henry," Rhonda said. "Not Levi Sanborn."

"Yes," Elizabeth nodded. "This is my brother, Henry Bullard."

"And I'm not a thief. Or a spy," Henry said. "Although someone has obviously been spying on *us*." He looked pointedly at Caroline.

Caroline's cheeks felt warm, despite the brisk November air. She knew it was wrong to eavesdrop, but she had done it for the most important of reasons—getting her papa's envelope back.

"I'm sorry," she said. "But you have to admit that your behavior has been suspicious from the very moment the stagecoach pulled up to the Eagle Tavern. And just now you disappeared around the privy as if you had something to hide."

Elizabeth and Henry exchanged a nervous glance. "I think we must tell them," Elizabeth said. Then she turned to Caroline and Rhonda. "We *have* been guarding a terrible secret, but it's not what you think."

Henry avoided meeting their eyes. "I'm a soldier—I was stationed in Sackets Harbor. And now I'm a deserter."

Rhonda gasped. "You deserted the army?" As the daughter of an army officer, she knew the gravity of such a crime. "How could you run away from your duty, especially when we're at war?"

"I didn't want to," Henry said. "Elizabeth sent a letter saying that my father was ill, and I was granted leave. He died before I could reach them. Elizabeth was left to run our farm by herself. I hoped to keep our farm going, so it would be there for me to go home to after the war. Elizabeth and I were working so hard to bring in the harvest that I was forced to delay my return to the army." The boy hung his head. "Without permission."

"Why didn't you go back when you sold the farm?" Rhonda asked.

"Punishment for desertion can be harsh," Henry said. "Even with a reason like mine. I should have asked to have my leave extended, but I was afraid the request would not be granted, so I just stayed away."

"The army came looking for him once," Elizabeth added. "I lied and said he wasn't there while he hid in the woods—so I'm guilty, too."

"I know what I did was wrong," Henry said. "But I've been afraid to go back. I decided to go to Albany with my sister and try to build a new life in the hope that the army would never look for me again."

*Poor Henry*, Caroline thought. *And poor Elizabeth!* When the British had imprisoned Caroline's papa early in the war, she had needed the rest of her family around her for comfort. She couldn't imagine what it must have been like for Henry to think about leaving Elizabeth alone on the farm when they had just lost their father. Caroline also knew all too well that taking care of a farm was the work of a family, not just one girl. Caroline thought she might have deserted the army, too, in that situation. Still, that didn't explain the pair's odd behavior.

"But . . . why did you follow us and hide in the woods instead of riding the coach with your sister?" she asked.

"When I saw Lieutenant Stockman sitting up front with Mr. Danforth, I panicked," Elizabeth said. "I was afraid he would recognize Henry. I was even afraid he would recognize our name—that's why I said I had been alone at the inn."

"I didn't want to leave Elizabeth completely on her own, so I borrowed a horse from one of our old neighbors, Mr. Kempers, and followed you," Henry added.

"Last night when I gave Henry the food, I told him that the officer had left the coach," Elizabeth explained.

"So it was safe for me to board the

stagecoach," Henry added. "We knew it would appear strange if I suddenly joined my sister, so we came up with a false name."

"But if you've decided to go back to the army, why do you have to hide who you are?" Rhonda asked. "And what about that horse? What have you done with it?"

Henry smiled. "Star knows this road well, so I took her out early this morning and sent her on her way just as I promised Mr. Kempers I would," he said. "She'll find her way home. As for calling myself Levi—I only decided over breakfast that I would go back to Sackets Harbor and face my captain. But I don't want to risk getting caught until Elizabeth is safely in the hands of our mother's friend, Mrs. Vandekerk. As soon as she's settled, I'll go back and accept my punishment."

"What made you change your mind?" Caroline asked.

"Perley Annable," Henry answered. "He's a brave man. He is so proud to have served his country and so determined to get well so that he can return to the navy. It made me ashamed of what I had done."

"You deserted to help me," Elizabeth said. "And to try to save our farm. That's nothing to be ashamed of."

Caroline agreed. She was moved by the young man's story and his willingness to accept responsibility for what he had done.

"I'm truly sorry for your troubles, and for accusing you wrongly," Caroline said. Her heart ached for the Bullards, but the need to find Papa's documents still pressed on her.

"Have either of you seen anything at all that might help me find out who took my father's envelope?" she asked. "It's very important that I find it!"

Caroline's heart thudded as she waited for the Bullards to answer. Finally, Henry shook his head. "I was too busy trying not to be seen to notice anything of value to you."

"And I was thinking only of Henry," added Elizabeth.

Caroline wanted to weep. Minutes ago, she'd

been so sure that Elizabeth and her young man were the thieves. Now she was no closer at all to getting Papa's envelope back.

Caroline and the Bullards quietly wished each other well, and then Caroline and Rhonda trudged back toward the inn.

"I'm sorry we didn't find your papa's papers, or my locket," Rhonda said. "But I have to admit that I'm relieved Elizabeth and her brother aren't guilty of stealing them. They're both such nice people."

Caroline nodded, silently scolding herself. Both she and Rhonda had been mistaken about Elizabeth and her brother, but her mistake had been worse.

"Let's see if Mr. Danforth has returned," Rhonda said, trying to be encouraging. "When we tell him about Mr. Herrick's doll and the handbill, he can help us make sense of it. Maybe he can even persuade Mr. Herrick to give everyone back their things. The law will certainly go easier on him if he does."

Caroline bit her lip. "What if I'm as wrong

about Mr. Herrick as I was about Elizabeth and Henry?"

"Don't give up yet," Rhonda said. "You told me that you were convinced the thief is one of our party. If that's true, then I'm sure we'll find him."

"I hope so," Caroline said. She pulled open the door to the inn and promised herself she would not give up until Papa's envelope was back in her hands.

# 13

# SERIOUS CHARGES

As Caroline and Rhonda stepped into the
dining room, Mary was coming out of the
kitchen. She held a bucket in her hands, and
her face was pinched with fear. They could
hear Mrs. Wendell shouting after her from the
kitchen.

"Stop being foolish, Mary, and do as you're
told," she said. "Those pigs need to be fed."

"Yes, ma'am," Mary said, her voice trembling.

Caroline hated to delay talking to Mr. Danforth
even for a moment, but she had been looking
for a chance to ask Mary whether she'd seen Mr.
Herrick nearby when the pigs had seemed to
speak. And Mary was clearly frightened to go
back to the pigpen. Caroline thought she could
put her mind at ease.

"Would you like us to come with you to feed the pigs?" Caroline asked.

"Oh, yes, miss," Mary said, her shoulders slumping with relief. "If those pigs start talking again, I don't know what I'll do. Everyone thinks it was a prank, but I saw those pigs talk. If there was a boy sitting in the middle of them trying to fool me, I would have seen him."

"I believe you," Caroline said.

Mary looked at her in surprise. "You do?"

"I think someone—someone with a special talent for voices—made it seem as if the sound came right from the middle of the pigs. I can't prove it yet, but I'm going to try," Caroline promised.

On the way to the barn, she and Rhonda asked Mary if she had seen anyone nearby when she fed the pigs the day before.

"Just the big, bossy gentleman—Mr. Jencks," Mary said.

They came to the barn, and Mary peeked inside, jumping with fright when one of the pigs began to snort at the sight of her.

"Here, I'll take the bucket," Caroline said. "I think the pig knows it's going to be fed."

Mary watched nervously while Caroline dumped the slops into the pigs' trough. The animals scampered over and stuck their snouts into the scraps, snorting and snuffling while they nudged each other out of the way to get to the best bits.

"What about Mr. Herrick?" Rhonda asked. "Did you see him in the yard when you came to feed the pigs yesterday?"

Mary shook her head no, but then her brow creased. "Wait—as I was carrying my buckets, I did pass him. He was showing a magic trick to the little boy."

"Did he follow you?" Caroline asked. "It's very important."

Mary frowned again. "I suppose he could have," she said. "Once those pigs started talking, I didn't see anything else."

Caroline and Rhonda exchanged a nod. Caroline realized that Mr. Herrick was the only one she couldn't remember seeing in the barn after Mary had yelled. *Maybe because he was at the stagecoach, stealing our things!*

"Let's go find Mr. Danforth," Caroline said.

While Mary carried her bucket back to the kitchen, the girls hurried to the ladies' parlor, only to learn that Mr. Danforth had not yet returned. Mrs. Wendell pointed them in the direction of the wheelwright's shop.

"He'll go there first," she said. "Tell him I'll keep a plate warm if he's not back in time for noon dinner. You two try to get back here in time, too."

"We will, Mrs. Wendell," Caroline promised.

The girls ran down the road to the wheelwright's shop, but it was cold and empty. Disappointed, they turned back to the inn. They were nearly there when a horse trotted up behind them. It was Mr. Danforth's, but the constable was not with him. *Oh, no,* Caroline thought. They needed the constable's help to arrest Mr. Herrick, and they needed it as soon as possible.

"Whoa, Blackie," Mr. Danforth said. "Morning, girls. I have good news. The wheelwright will be back shortly and will get right to work on fixing the stagecoach. I expect to be on the road before first light tomorrow. And the constable will be joining us before we depart. He's searching for evidence on the road between here and Utica. Someone might have seen something."

"Good!" said Caroline, relieved that the constable was on his way. She poured out her story to Mr. Danforth—beginning with the thefts she'd heard about in Sackets Harbor and Mr. Herrick's suspicious last-minute dash to the stagecoach. She filled him in on her theory that a thief had distracted them twice—with the bobcat cry and with the talking pigs. Finding the ventriloquist's doll, she said, had led to that theory.

"We believe that a ventriloquist drew us away from the stagecoach in order to steal our things," Caroline said, her words tumbling out in a rush.

"And that leads us to Mr. Herrick," Rhonda said. "He is a professional entertainer, so it must be him. Who else could it be?"

"We can't let him get away," Caroline said. "Mr. Jencks's report and Papa's papers would be very helpful to the enemy. The British would pay a lot of money for them. And," she added, looking at her friend, "Rhonda could never replace her locket."

Caroline held her breath as Mr. Danforth thought over all she and Rhonda had said. His face was lined with worry and sadness. Finally, he spoke.

"These are very serious charges," he said. "I've known Mr. Herrick for many years. I've driven him from town to town on my stagecoach and watched him bring happiness to people. I've never seen him exhibit this talent for throwing his voice. I don't believe—"

# Serious Charges

Caroline couldn't help interrupting. "Maybe it's a new skill of his," she said. "How else would you explain the handbill we found yesterday, and the doll Jackson found? Yesterday morning Mr. Jencks said that there was a thief about and that he was believed to be a traveling entertainer. And Mr. Herrick's own handbill says that he is a ventriloquist."

"Where is this handbill?" Mr. Danforth asked. "I'd like to see it before we speak to Mr. Herrick."

"It's in our bedchamber," Caroline answered. "I'll go and get it."

"I need to take Blackie back to the stable," Mr. Danforth said. "Meet me there."

Caroline and Rhonda ran back to the inn, pausing only to answer Mrs. Potter's question about whether they had found Mr. Danforth. Then they raced upstairs, hoping Jackson hadn't found the doll already.

To her relief, Caroline found the doll and the handbill under her pillow where she had left them. She slipped them under her cloak and hurried back downstairs, tiptoeing so that Mrs. Potter wouldn't call them into the parlor again.

Finding Mr. Danforth in the stable, they handed over the evidence.

"This is very curious," Mr. Danforth said, examining the handbill. "I've never seen Mr. Herrick perform under any name but his own. Why would he have a handbill calling himself The Great Nicolas?"

"I can't answer that," said Caroline. "But you can see he lists one of his entertainments as ventriloquism. Who else but a ventriloquist could have made you think we screamed for help in the woods, or made Mary believe the pigs talked?"

Mr. Danforth sighed and shook his head. "I find this very hard to believe about my old friend. He's never been anything but forthright."

Caroline understood the driver's disappointment. She couldn't help liking Mr. Herrick, too. "Shouldn't we inform the constable?" she asked.

Mr. Danforth nodded grimly. "I'd like to talk to Mr. Herrick first—but privately. There may be a very good explanation for this," he said, indicating the doll and the handbill. "I won't have a man's reputation destroyed on mere suspicion."

Caroline knew that Mr. Danforth was right, but it was hard to imagine what Mr. Herrick's explanation could be. The girls and Mr. Danforth had just left the stable when they saw Mr. Herrick striding across the yard toward them.

"Peter, I heard you were back," Mr. Herrick said with a smile. "What's the report from the wheelwright?"

"We'll be on the road tomorrow morning," Mr. Danforth said.

"And the constable?" Mr. Herrick asked.

"He's on his way," the driver answered uncomfortably. The girls looked at each other, unwilling to meet Mr. Herrick's friendly gaze.

Mr. Herrick took in the group's grave expressions. "Why so somber?" he asked. "Surely nothing else has gone wrong."

Mr. Danforth drew a deep breath. "Can you explain these things?" he asked, handing

Mr. Herrick the handbill and showing him the doll. "We believe they belong to the thief who has been plaguing us."

Caroline studied Mr. Herrick's face as he unfolded the handbill and read it, but she saw no sign of guilt or surprise. Instead, he only nodded slightly, pressed his lips together, and then returned the handbill. "I suspected as much," he told Mr. Danforth grimly. "I thought our thief might be a ventriloquist. But I couldn't confront him without proof—proof I've been trying very hard to find."

Caroline wasn't surprised that Mr. Herrick would deny being the thief, but she was stunned by what he'd just said. Was he suggesting that the ventriloquist and thief was *another* of the passengers?

"The ventriloquist isn't you?" she asked. "This isn't your handbill?"

"Mine?" Mr. Herrick said with surprise. "No. I believe this belongs to Mr. Jencks. And I believe he is the thief!"

# 14

# A Trap to Catch a Thief

"Mr. *Jencks*?" Caroline blinked in confusion. "How could Mr. Jencks be our thief? He was one of the thief's targets."

"He's an important man," Rhonda added. "He works for Governor Tompkins."

"So he *says*," Mr. Herrick replied. "But what proof have we? The facts he's gathering have mostly to do with the prosperity of the villages we've traveled through. I'll wager he simply wants to know what there is to steal. And he's clever enough to make himself seem like an innocent victim."

Mr. Danforth looked at Mr. Herrick skeptically. "I know he accused you of theft unjustly. Be careful you aren't doing the same to him."

"Yes, of course," Mr. Herrick agreed. "But

I've been watching him, and there's something amiss. I believe he's used me as a way to set the stage for his own thievery."

Mr. Herrick told the group about a rash of thefts in the area, all connected to a traveling entertainer. "I can't tell you how many times I've been questioned by constables over the past months. I've been run out of towns that I've performed in for years," he said. "That's why I'm joining the theater troupe in Albany. I can no longer make a living on the road, doing what I love to do.

"I've long believed that someone was using other entertainers' performances, including mine, as a way to steal from large groups of people," Mr. Herrick went on. "Since that episode in the woods when Miss Hathaway's locket was stolen, I've suspected it was Mr. Jencks."

"Why?" Caroline asked.

"I thought that the screams in the woods might be the work of a ventriloquist—and that it might be the same person who's been stealing throughout these parts," Mr. Herrick said.

"Mr. Jencks fit the description of a traveling entertainer I had heard about, but the man performed under a different name."

"The Great Nicolas?" Rhonda asked.

Mr. Herrick nodded. "Yes. That and others."

"And so you've been following Mr. Jencks since Rhonda's necklace disappeared, hoping to catch him stealing again?" Caroline asked. She didn't mention that she had suspected Mr. Herrick of wanting to steal Mr. Jencks's report for the governor.

"Yes, but yesterday, just as Mr. Jencks entered the inn yard, Jackson begged me for a magic trick. By the time I turned to follow Mr. Jencks, he had disappeared and that poor serving girl was screaming about the talking pigs."

Caroline's eyes widened. "Mr. Jencks was the last of the group to join us in the barn," she said. "Just as he was the last to find us in the woods yesterday."

"I became convinced of his guilt when we heard the boys' laughter from the woods," Mr. Herrick continued. "Mr. Jencks turned his back on us and walked away just before we heard the laughter."

"He pretended that he works for the governor just to appear innocent?" Rhonda asked.

"Who would you suspect less than an agent of Governor Tompkins?" Caroline said. She thought for a moment. "When does the constable arrive?"

"Later today," Mr. Danforth replied.

"We must tell the constable everything as soon as he gets here!" said Caroline. "I must get Papa's papers back."

"Hold on a minute, Caroline," Mr. Danforth said. "I want to get your property back, but all we have are suspicions. We have no proof. Mr. Jencks submitted himself to a search yesterday, and we found nothing. And if by chance he really is an agent of the governor, he could have me—and possibly your father—severely punished for accusing him falsely."

While Mr. Danforth spoke, Mr. Herrick gazed off into the distance, as if considering something. "During yesterday's search, Jencks emptied his coat pockets," Mr. Herrick said finally. "But many magicians have secret pockets to conceal things for sleight-of-hand tricks. It's likely he has a secret pocket in his greatcoat where he hides stolen goods until he can transfer them to his valise."

"He never takes that coat off," Rhonda said.

"And he always carries his bag with him, too," Caroline added.

Mr. Herrick nodded. "Jencks is the reason I didn't want to perform tonight. I'm afraid he's going to use my act as a distraction to pick the pockets of Mr. Wendell's customers. He may even use his ventriloquist tricks again."

Caroline felt sure Mr. Herrick was right. But she also understood that without proof, there was nothing the constable could do. "We have to find a way to keep Mr. Jencks from robbing more people," she said. "And we have to get proof of what he's done."

"Which means we'll need to find a way to conduct a thorough search of his coat and his valise before he suspects anything," said Mr. Danforth.

Caroline's eyes met Mr. Herrick's, and she suddenly got an idea. "Maybe we can catch him in the act!"

It took only a few minutes for Caroline to explain her plan, and for Mr. Herrick to come up with a magic trick that would lay a trap for the thief.

By late afternoon, everything was in place for Mr. Herrick's performance. Caroline's stomach bubbled with worried excitement as people began to arrive from as far as two villages away. The tables in the dining room had been carried out, and chairs were lined up for the audience. But there were so many guests that many men stood at the back of the room. Caroline watched Mr. Jencks move among them—shaking hands, patting men on the back, and making small talk.

Even though she was looking for it, Caroline didn't catch him picking even one pocket. *Could I be wrong?* she wondered. *Could this all be a huge mistake?*

Then it was time for Mr. Herrick's performance to begin. He took his place in front of the

door leading to the kitchen. He had stretched
a rope from one side of the dining room to the
other, to separate the "stage" from the audience.

Rhonda and Caroline, her knees shaking a
little beneath her skirt, took places behind the rope
at either side of the entertainer. They would be his
assistants for the evening. Mr. Danforth stood in
the doorway leading to the front of the inn.

Caroline was too focused on Mr. Jencks to
enjoy Mr. Herrick's act, but the audience clapped
loudly after every trick. He began by singing a
happy song and dancing about while he juggled
three, four, and then five balls, dropping none
of them. He teased the audience by *almost* dropping the balls twice. Then he caught them all
with a flourish and began making coins and
marbles appear in funny places on people
throughout the room.

Next came a series of rope tricks. Caroline's
eyes darted from Mr. Herrick to Mr. Jencks.
She didn't want to let the thief out of her
sight, but she was fascinated by Mr. Herrick's
entertainments.

He made the rope disappear and asked
Rhonda to fetch him the bowl of eggs that
Mrs. Wendell had provided earlier, along
with the hornpipe that sat on top of the bowl.
Caroline watched him select one egg and place
it on the table in front of him. When he played
a tune, the egg twisted and rolled as if it were
dancing!

*How could that be?* she wondered. As quick as
a wink Mr. Herrick finished, and Caroline was
no closer to discovering the trick behind this feat
than she was to discovering how he had invisibly
mended her rope.

Next Mr. Herrick borrowed Mr. Danforth's
pocket watch, turned it into a turnip, and then
back into a watch!

*How did he do that?* Caroline was so captivated
by the trick that she almost forgot to keep her eye
on Mr. Jencks. Even Mr. Jencks applauded and
shouted with the others.

Finally, Mr. Herrick looked from Rhonda to
Caroline with a nod. It was time to lay their trap.

"For my next trick, I ask all my stagecoach

companions to take the chairs in the front row," Mr. Herrick announced.

Mrs. Potter, Jackson, and Elizabeth Bullard were already in the front row. Mr. Wendell's other customers changed seats with the other stagecoach passengers. Caroline and Rhonda stepped over the rope and into the audience to direct Perley Annable and Henry Bullard to their new seats. They saved the chair in the very middle of the row for Mr. Jencks.

"I am too tall," he said, backing away. "I will block the view of the ladies behind me."

"I insist, Mr. Jencks," Mr. Herrick announced. "You are essential to my grand finale."

# 15

## BEWARE THE MAGICIAN!

Mr. Jencks continued to protest but finally allowed himself to be led to the front of the room to join the others. He dropped into his seat and set his valise at his feet.

Caroline stayed on the audience's side of the rope while Rhonda took her place beside Mr. Herrick. Caroline swallowed and caught Rhonda's eye with a nod. They had to be ready to act fast.

Mr. Herrick jumped over the rope and strolled among the stagecoach passengers, making funny remarks. He produced another marble from Jackson's nose, making him giggle. Perley Annable's pocket yielded Mrs. Potter's handkerchief, and a playing card seemed to rise from Elizabeth Bullard's collar by itself.

Mr. Jencks, Caroline noticed, kept his arms folded over his coat. His feet were planted solidly on either side of his valise. His eyes followed Mr. Herrick suspiciously as the magician weaved among the group as if casting spells. Suddenly, Mr. Herrick snapped his fingers just behind Mr. Jencks's left ear, and a flame burned for an instant.

Startled, Mr. Jencks jumped to his feet. Anger flashed across his face.

Mr. Herrick turned to Mr. Jencks with a sly smile. "Too close to the fire, sir?" he asked.

That was Caroline's cue. She snatched Mr. Jencks's valise and slid it under the rope to Rhonda.

"My bag!" Mr. Jencks shouted, but Mr. Herrick acted as if he hadn't heard. He just kept up his witty banter with the audience and hopped nimbly over the rope to join Rhonda. Caroline followed him. Mr. Jencks glared darkly at the three of them.

"The time has come for my final act of astonishment this evening," he announced. He chose another egg from the bowl and held it above his head. "This is an ordinary egg, is it not?" he asked Mrs. Wendell.

She nodded. "Plucked from the chicken coop this morning."

"I will fry this egg, using neither fat nor fire," Mr. Herrick announced. "And to prove there's no trickery involved, I will use this bag of Mr. Jencks's to do so."

"I must object," Mr. Jencks said, rising to his feet. "My belongings—"

"I assure you, your belongings will be unharmed," Mr. Herrick said.

Mr. Jencks reached for the bag, but he was stopped by the rope between the audience and the stage. His size and heavy overcoat made it impossible for him to leap over the rope as Mr. Herrick had.

"What secrets does the bag contain?" asked Mr. Herrick, holding the bag out of reach. His voice pulled the whole room into the question.

Caroline could see the tension in Mr. Jencks's face. He smiled and sat down again, but his teeth were clenched tight and a vein in his forehead throbbed.

"My assistants will guard your things," Mr. Herrick said. With one quick motion, he opened the bag and turned it upside down. Mr. Jencks's belongings fell to the table.

Caroline scanned the table, expecting to see Papa's envelope and Rhonda's locket. Instead, she saw a shaving brush, a few pieces of clothing, and a messy sheaf of papers that were clearly not Papa's. Her heart sank, and she looked at Mr. Herrick in alarm. Had their plan gone terribly wrong? But his face was calm.

He held the bag open and showed it to the audience. "As you can see," he pronounced, "the bag is empty. No trickery here." He paused dramatically.

Caroline could hardly bear the silence that filled the room. *What was he doing?*

Then Mr. Herrick lifted the bag to his ear and shook it. "But what's this?" he asked. "Do I hear something?"

Quickly, he reached into the bag and tugged.

"A false bottom!" he announced. "What's hidden underneath?"

Suddenly, a deep, hollow laugh bounced around the room. It seemed to come from the ceiling.

Most of the audience laughed uneasily, believing that the sound was part of Mr. Herrick's act.

Then a deep voice boomed from the ceiling. "Beware the magician," it said.

A woman screamed.

"A ghost!" Jackson shouted.

Again, the unearthly laughter came. Panicked, people in the audience leaped from their seats and rushed toward the door where Mr. Danforth stood. He let them pass, but he kept his post at the door. Caroline noticed that his eyes, like those of Mr. Herrick, didn't leave Mr. Jencks.

As people raced for the door, the ghostly voice continued to speak. "I come from beyond the grave to warn you. Beware the magician!" it boomed.

Caroline climbed up onto the table that Mr. Herrick used for his entertainments. She

watched Mr. Jencks try to slip out along with
the rest of the crowd. Mr. Danforth blocked him.
Mr. Jencks spun on his heel and pushed his
way toward the dining room's back door, but
Mr. Herrick had already planted himself there.

"We're onto your tricks," Mr. Herrick said.
"You can't fool us this time."

Mr. Jencks's bag was on the table at Caroline's
feet. She picked it up and peered into the deep
secret compartment Mr. Herrick had pulled
open. There, among a tangle of other items, was
Papa's envelope! And Rhonda's necklace, too.
Caroline grabbed them and held them tight.

In the midst of the chaos, a tall man with an
air of authority strode into the room. Caroline
heard someone call him Constable.

"That man is a thief," Mr. Herrick announced,
pointing to Mr. Jencks. "We've just found stolen
property in his valise. If you check his greatcoat,
I believe you'll find hidden pockets holding valuables that he took from tonight's guests."

Mr. Jencks looked around the room desperately and seemed to shrink in size as he realized

there was no way out. The ghostly voice came again from the ceiling, but this time it sounded weak and halfhearted. Caroline could see his lips twitch with every sound he made.

As Mr. Herrick, Mr. Danforth, and the constable circled him, Mr. Jencks seemed to see that it was pointless to struggle. He slipped off his coat and handed it to the constable.

"Do what you will," he muttered.

Rhonda looked up at Caroline and noticed the leather envelope in her friend's hand. Her eyes filled with tears. "You've done it," she said. "You got your papa's envelope back."

Caroline nodded and sat down on the edge of the table. She pressed the locket into Rhonda's palm, closing her fingers around it, and then pulled her friend into a hug. "*We've* done it."

After being told of Mr. Jencks's crimes and how he had fooled the audience, Mr. and

Mrs. Wendell hurried out to calm their frightened guests. Caroline and Rhonda stayed behind to listen as the constable and Mr. Danforth questioned the thief.

The constable pulled stolen items one by one out of the deep pocket in the lining of Mr. Jencks's coat. There were several pocket watches, handfuls of coins and folding money, some necklaces, and even a pair of spectacles. Caroline figured most of them probably belonged to the people who'd come to watch Mr. Herrick's show. Many of the things hidden under the false bottom of Mr. Jencks's valise—stolen earlier in his travels—could not be immediately returned, but Mrs. Potter's earrings were among them.

Looking over the heap of stolen goods, Caroline understood that Mr. Jencks was a terribly greedy man. He'd surely have sold Papa's papers to the British as soon as he could. She shivered at the thought.

Caroline and Rhonda stood arm in arm as the constable led Mr. Jencks away. Caroline couldn't help feeling a little sad for him. His life was as false as the bottom in his valise—and as empty now, too. Caroline's own life felt so full of things far more important than money—her family, her good friend Rhonda, and her home on her beloved Lake Ontario.

Caroline's eyes fell on Henry Bullard and his sister. He was a young man who had made a wrong choice, but for the right reasons. Like Mr. Jencks, he had deceived people, but he had done so out of love for his family. That was a reason Caroline could understand. She hated to think about the punishment Henry would face when he turned himself in to the army.

"I wish there were a way we could help Henry," she told Rhonda.

Rhonda followed her gaze. "Maybe I can," she said. "I'll write to my father and tell him Henry's story. When he hears why Henry left the army and how sorry he is, I'm sure he'll try to help."

With that matter as settled as it could be for now, Caroline turned her attention to helping

Mr. Herrick pack his magic equipment. She lifted his hornpipe off the table, and to her surprise, an egg rose up with it. Examining it, she could see that there were tiny holes on each end of the egg. Mr. Herrick had emptied it of its contents, threaded a horsehair through the egg, and attached the horsehair to his hornpipe. Like a puppet on a string, the egg would move whenever Mr. Herrick moved the hornpipe. Even from a few feet away, the horsehair would be impossible to see. *No wonder it danced to the music,* she thought. *How clever!*

She caught Mr. Herrick's eye, and he brought his finger to his lips with a smile.

Caroline nodded, smiling in return. She would keep the magician's secret.

Before dawn the next morning, the passengers gathered in front of the inn while the stable boys helped Mr. Danforth harness the horses.

# THE TRAVELER'S TRICK

Mr. Herrick drew Caroline aside. "As my assistant, you are entitled to learn one more magic trick," he said. "What will it be?"

Caroline's eyes lit up. "The rope trick!" she said. "I'd so love to be able to amaze Papa with it."

For the next few minutes, Caroline watched intently over Mr. Herrick's shoulder as he looped the rope in a special way inside his hand and cut the loop of rope that poked out from his fist. Then he wrapped the rope around his hand, waved his penknife over the rope, slipped the knife back into his pocket, and revealed an uncut rope!

"I think I understand," Caroline said slowly. "You're not really cutting the rope in the middle. You're only cutting a tiny piece off the end of the rope. But no one can see that because you're hiding it inside your fist."

"That's it," Mr. Herrick said, handing her the rope and the knife. "Now you try."

Her brow furrowed in concentration, Caroline repeated each step of the trick. Then, waving the penknife over the rope, she unwound a whole, uncut rope!

"You did magic!" Jackson said, running over.

Caroline hadn't realized anyone was watching. She knew she had done the trick much too slowly. Anyone watching carefully would have guessed how she had done it. But Jackson's words made her feel good. "I'm going to keep practicing," she told Mr. Herrick. "I'll be as fast as you by the time I get home to Sackets Harbor."

She was about to try again when Mr. Danforth called "All aboard!" and everyone hurried to the stagecoach.

The driver gave Caroline a hand up onto the coach and then climbed up himself. She sat on one side of the driver on the front bench, Papa's papers safely tucked in the carpetbag at her feet and her rope in her hand. Rhonda took the other side, her gold locket around her neck, glinting in the light from the rising sun.

Then the driver, with a salute to Mr. Wendell and the wheelwright, snapped his whip over the ears of the lead horse. Once again, they were trotting down the road to Albany.

# LOOKING BACK

## A PEEK INTO THE PAST

*Albany, New York, in 1805. Because travel was difficult in Caroline's time, many children grew up without ever seeing such a big town.*

For girls growing up on the frontier, like Caroline, a visit to a city was truly a special event. Today, a 180-mile trip like the one she takes from her village of Sackets Harbor to Albany, New York, would mean just a few hours in a car. For Caroline, the same journey meant three bumpy, exhausting days in a horse-drawn stagecoach.

*Travelers jounced along dirt roads in crowded stagecoaches.*

Many coaches in Caroline's time had no windows or walls. Only leather curtains sheltered passengers from wind, rain, cold, and dust from the road.

*A coach sets off from an inn for a day's ride through dark, lonely forests.*

The benches were hard and sometimes crowded. Coaches also carried packages for people who lived along their routes, and baggage sometimes took up so much floor space that there was no place for travelers to rest their feet.

Stagecoach trips were risky as well as uncomfortable. Coaches could tip over on rough, rutted roads. When frightened, horses might bolt and cause crashes. And if a coach broke down, there was only the driver—or the passengers themselves—to make repairs.

Although robberies on the road were not as common as accidents, stagecoaches could make inviting targets for thieves.

*Stagecoach drivers often put passengers' money and important papers in a leather case like this for safekeeping.*

*Passengers get a warm farewell as their coach departs. Their luggage is stowed on the back—an easy target for thieves.*

Travelers had to carry enough funds for the journey, plus whatever money and valuables they would need when they reached their destination. A thief could hide along a route and snatch bags from the back of a slow-moving coach without even being seen. By the time passengers noticed that their bags were missing at the next stop, the culprit would be long gone!

Despite its hazards, stagecoach travel could be great fun. Travelers sang songs and carried on lively conversations about books, politics, and war. Passengers talked about their lives and, over the course of a long trip, might get to know one other well. Some stagecoach drivers amused travelers with jokes and tall tales. Colonel Silas May, a driver in New Hampshire, entertained his passengers by playing tunes on the bugle he also used for signaling other drivers and announcing the coach's arrival at roadside taverns.

*A colorful tavern sign*

After many miles on the road, the sight of a tavern's distinctive sign might also lift a traveler's spirits. During Caroline's time, roadside taverns were a bit like the roadside diners and motels of today; there, travelers would find the warmth of a fire, a refreshing drink, a hot meal, and a place to sleep. They could not, however, expect to have a room to themselves—

*Taverns were popular stops for local people as well as travelers. A stagecoach might pull in next to cows and covered farm wagons.*

and often not even their own bed. It wasn't unusual to be shaken awake in the middle of the night and told to slide over so a new guest could crawl in beside you!

Taverns were important not just to travelers but also to the people who lived near them. A tavern might function as a post office, a store, and a place to buy and sell horses, hear gossip, and play games like checkers. Some taverns even had their own bowling lanes.

Taverns also hosted traveling artists and entertainers, including painters, musicians, puppeteers, and performers. Traveling entertainers

were welcomed, but they weren't always trusted. In small villages, magicians were especially suspect, because people didn't always understand that the tricks they

*A lively tavern in 1814*

performed were just illusions—not truly magic or supernatural. Still, when a traveling magic show arrived at a local tavern, it was sure to draw a crowd. Imagine how exciting it might be, in a tiny village where nothing much changed from day to

**FEMALE ELEPHANT.**

THE only Elephant now in America, is in this town, and may be seen at Mrs. Hodg-son's tavern to-day, and Monday next. Admittance 25 cents, for all over twelve years old—from that to five, 12½ cents. Dover, Oct. 7, 1815.

*Taverns hosted all kinds of unusual attractions— even exotic animals!*

day, to see a potato suddenly turn into a pocket watch or a coin seem to vanish into thin air!

*Traveling magic shows became popular long before Caroline's time. This magician dazzles a tavern crowd in the 1700s.*

# About the Author

Laurie Calkhoven has traveled by plane, train, car, bus, subway, and bicycle, but never by stagecoach. She grew up in New Jersey, where her earliest passions were reading and writing. During long family car trips, she would while away the hours by making up stories about the people and places she passed along the way.

Today she lives in New York City, where she makes up stories for a living. In addition to *The Traveler's Tricks*, she has written five novels in American Girl's Innerstar University series, including *The New Girl* and *Project Friendship*.